The Unicorn
An Historical Fantasy

*Keep the faith always,
you won't be
disappointed!
To John Bosworth*

JOHN BOOS, MAFR

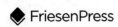 FriesenPress

Suite 300 - 990 Fort St
Victoria, BC, V8V 3K2
Canada

www.friesenpress.com

Copyright © 2020 by John Boos
First Edition — 2020

Illustrated by Tony Boos

All events related are from the happenings of history, and any relationship to living folk is merely co-incidental.

ISBN
978-1-5255-6457-4 (Hardcover)
978-1-5255-6458-1 (Paperback)
978-1-5255-6459-8 (eBook)

1. JUVENILE FICTION, HISTORICAL, ANCIENT CIVILIZATIONS

Distributed to the trade by The Ingram Book Company

Table of Contents

FORWARD

A Unicorn?

No one to my knowledge has ever seen a real live Unicorn. And yet, legends of this fabulous horse with a spiral horn on its forehead exist in many countries, and have been around for many hundreds of years. Anthropologists and sociologists have written about the fascination he holds for man, painters and poets have had their say. Yet he remains in the realm of myth.

But myths die hard, and seem to be necessary to give an aura of magic, of otherworldliness, to the humdrum greyness of our lives. To help us to imagine, to go beyond harsh reality. And to this the Unicorn is no exception. He is there to fill a gap in our emptiness....

In this little book – an historical fantasy using real facts as foundation, together with a sprinkling from great works of Faith – the Unicorn is seen as a traveller through time and cultures. Blessed with incredible gifts, his adventures range from prehistory through certain important historic eras, right up to our present time.

Though his interests concentrate on the European mainland, yet we find him in many other parts of the world, gathering information and reflecting on his experiences as he moves along. We find him in the Near and Far East, Africa, and even in the Americas, inviting us to share in all his adventures.

As it would have been clearly impossible for him to have had knowledge of all historical experience, it has been necessary to bring to light the most important bits which attracted his attention, the rest being introduced as supplementary information. He hopes that his adventures will encourage further historical investigation on the part of his readers, in this fascinating world of ours.

The Unicorn does not create history, he lives it, he breathes it. Which is why, though it is history, it is also fantasy as seen through his eyes, and is meant to be taken as such. And he is the greatest fantasy of all.

And when we look upwards to Little World, perhaps one night we may see the Blue Light coming down once again, and the Unicorn will continue his adventures among us.

Welcome to the Story of the One-Horn, Uni, the Unicorn.

Part 1

CHAPTER 1
Before: Big World

When Big World was very, very young (a), steamy tropical forests covered most of its surface. Here and there, clumped together, standing by themselves or in long chains, huge volcanoes rumbled and exploded, spewing rivers of red and white-hot lava down into the valleys at their feet. By day lightning and storms lit up the sky, and at night the volcanoes continued to empty their liquid rock over the land, glowing in the dark sky and showing up the forests in their angry redness. Dark storm-clouds loomed overhead in unending rollers, and seemingly incessant rain pelted down in vast sheets upon the forests. Lakes were formed, overflowing into rivers which grew wider and wider before emptying themselves into the seas. At the end of the day no light shone in the sky. Little World hadn't yet arrived.

Ages passed, and strange creatures began to move through the forests and humid swamps. Insects with yard-long wingspans, toothed and feathered bird-like creatures with claws at their elbow-joints, multitudes of scorpions, millipedes, flies and roaches.

Overlording them all were the lizards. Small ones scuttled among the thick forests and the trunks of fallen trees, hunted by the larger. Gigantic long-necked ones ripped off the leaves from the tall trees on the banks of the rain-filled marshes. Their cumbersome bodies moved slowly on tree-trunk legs as they fed, returning to the marsh to rest in the bulk-supporting water.

Long-necked bats glided from tree to tree on their leather-skinned wings, swooping down suddenly to catch the scaly fish on the surface of the marsh, and to scrabble around for carrion.

In the open flat-lands the terrible raptors and thunder-lizards ripped off whole chunks of flesh from the sides of the slower-moving leaf-eaters. And in the warm seas, and in the rivers and marshes, roiled and fought and died monstrous fish and snakes and armoured reptiles. Such was Big World when it was young.

And so, the millions of years rolled on, Big World slowly turning in the emptiness of space, following its invisible path around Big Light. Millions of miles away, other Big Worlds swept along on their own ways, turning and spinning around Big Light and other worlds. Balls of molten rock, frozen matter and shining gases, later to be called stars and planets. In time Big Light would be called "Sun", and Big World, where Mankind would be born, would live, love, fight, and die, would become the "Earth". Mankind's Earth.

LITTLE WORLD

She came sweeping in from the furthest unknown reaches of outer space, a mass of globular rock, pockmarked, cratered and tortured by the millions of meteors flung at her in her lonely endless wanderings through the ages. No rivers flowed there, no beasts walked nor fought, no forests grew on the grey dust of her matt and lifeless surface. A dead little world, just about one-quarter the size of Big World, spinning almost directly in her path.

From millions of miles away Little World felt the pull of the mass of the bigger body, gradually speeding up as she was seized and drawn closer as the centuries passed. It seemed that a direct collision of the two was certain, but her speed and angle of approach were just fine enough for her to be grabbed and pulled in closer to Big World.

She struggled to escape from the terrible attraction, fighting desperately to continue on her accustomed wanderings. But she was not strong enough to speed off again into outer space, nor too weak to be pulled into a direct collision. She felt herself being pulled apart as her speed was slowly tamed and gradually controlled. She shuddered uncontrollably as huge rocks broke off and flew into the sky. Dust on her surface flew upwards in protesting clouds, disappearing in a trail as her main mass hurtled onwards, becoming less frequent as Big World's gravity slowed her down.

Gradually and agonisingly her path was bent and curved into a circle around Big World. Her speed slowed just enough and remained constant enough to be equal to the strength of the gravity pulling her inwards. Her wanderings were over.

She was still travelling at high speed, but now in a curved path. She began to circle Big World over and

over, hiding by day, coming out in her glory at night. Measuring the days, measuring the months, measuring the years and the centuries. Partner to Big World, changing him forever.

And so, the Moon was captured in full flight by the Earth, and the dull-witted monsters below would continue to feed at night in her pale gleam, oblivious to the importance of the drama that had taken place above them.

For Moon reflected Sun's light to Earth, and the harshness of the day with its steaming heat was tempered by the coolness of the night when Moon became Queen, and Earth was at rest (b).

But Moon had not come alone, with nothing to offer but her beauty at night.

In one of the craters facing Earth neat rows and layers of strange intensely-blue crystals came to life again under the rays of the Sun. They were all that was left of a great stellar civilisation, retaining in the structure of their cells the entirety of its vast history, its culture and its wisdom. They had been sent on their outward journey by the last survivors of these unknown Ancients. Now they had come to rest in orbit around the Earth, after all the untold distances and eons of time covered by the captured Moon.

Gradually the crystals began communicating among themselves and exchanging information, bringing into life and purpose again the energy and programmes which had long lay dormant. Now it was time for the Plan to be realised, and a brilliant blue glow soon lay over the rows and layers of crystals as their energies combined and interacted to bring their existence into meaning.

At times when Moon remained in Earth's shadow for a dark lunar month, the brilliant blue glow would streak outwards and downwards towards the Earth, hundreds of thousands of miles away.

The giant lizards far below would continue to fight and eat and die, generation after generation, while the intense beam would ceaselessly skim over mountain and marsh, play on the tall forest trees, reflect on the pools and rivers, lighting up the landscape in its strange glow. Moving on, as if looking for something..... looking for something.....

CHAPTER 2

During: Arrival

Dusk in a dark lunar month.

He felt her muscles pushing him along as her time drew near. The slippery liquid of the passage eased him along slowly, sweetly, surely, as the mare breathed in, gathering strength as she relaxed and then tensed her stomach muscles, to push again and again, feeling his body move within her.

His hind legs came free first, slippery and flopping onto the soft earth below as his body slowly followed. The forelegs were tucked together under his chest, and finally his head came free, eyes and mouth closed as he lay on the ground near his mother. For a while she rested at the side of her first-born. But soon she got up and stood over him as he lay motionless and wet on the ground. She licked him and nudged the still body, and soon the tiny foal responded to the licking and nudging. His lungs filled with life-giving air, and he struggled uncertainly to his feet and looked around at the world with liquid eyes of wonder. A very special horse had been born into the world.

It was then that the Blue Light from above found him. It played softly over his wobbly body, caressed his flanks, travelled up the shining back, found the dark questioning eyes and tiny ears, and came to rest on his forehead. And there it stayed.

The mare looked on, puzzled. Her maternal instinct urged her to nurse her foal, and she whinnied in encouragement. But he stood trembling as the beam focussed its blue point on his forehead. For long minutes, which stretched into the hours of dawn, the foal stood there unmoving, feeling the strange tingling in the bones of his forehead where the beam rested. Then with the dawn it dimmed and went away.

The foal whinnied softly as the Blue Light dimmed and disappeared. He came up to the mare and nudged her side, then closed his eyes in rapture as he suckled greedily. Then he lay down and slept. It had been a long night, and he had just been born.

The Blue Light returned the following night, finding him unerringly in the clearing. Caressing and warming as it played over his body, it came to rest again on the little forehead, where the foal felt again the tingling feeling and warmth as the beam did its work.

This went on for every night of the lunar month, the foal eagerly anticipating the visit of the blue light, standing perfectly motionless as the strange ritual was played out.

Little by little the bones on his forehead began to pucker and stand out, and soon a little knob appeared which grew as the pulling of the beam became stronger, forming a little horn which showed itself through the soft fur. In the course of the month the horn grew and slowly turned upon itself three times in spiral whorls, ending in a point, firmly seated on his forehead.

At the month's end the beam's visits were coming to an end, and the mare whinnied impatiently as she waited for the strange encounter to end, but the foal with the little knurled horn on his forehead paid no attention to her anxious moans. His body too had changed, growing three times faster than nature allowed. Soon he was up to his mother's shoulder, and stamped his feet and snorted with impatience as the Light-beam increased its power, as though to hasten its effect on his growth.

His mother presented her side again for him to nurse, but now he was too big to do so, and there was his horn…..His coat of cream-coloured duff had now changed to a glossy white, the liquid eyes seemed to contain wells of ancient wisdom as yet unborn, and the whorled horn on his forehead stood out, as if waving a banner, The hooves shone as if polished by the brilliance of the Moon.

The beam of Blue Light was changing now, broadening from intense concentration to a wide circular swathe, covering the whole gleaming body of the Foal-with-the-Horn. It began to pulse in rapid waves, becoming even more liquid and alive as if impatient with its own internal urgency, giving its strength, giving its wisdom, giving its life. The foal stood still, understanding that he must be still until the Light's work were done.

The beam from far above finally began to grow dim and almost transparent as daylight began creeping down the slopes of the volcanoes. Gradually it became nothing

more than a faint blue haze, finally wisping away altogether as Sun's razing brightness entered their clearing. The month was over.

In their crater far above, the blue crystals had done their work well, just as the Ancients had planned. They had brought and implanted the wisdom of another world into the only creature capable of receiving and making use of it. And now they must hide and wait. Their time would come again. They had no fear of waiting….it was their custom….

An order went out from the crystals, and soon loose chunks of rock and clouds of grey dust on the crater's sides began stirring and rolling down to the bottom, dragging along others with them. Soon the whole surface of the rows and layers of the crystals were hidden under a thin cover of grey dust, through which the Sun's rays would penetrate and recharge. There they would remain. To wait….

The foal whinnied softly as the Light dimmed and died and disappeared. He came up to his mother and nudged her side, as if to console her for his apparent neglect. Among the many gifts he had received from the beam was that of Thought-Speech, which he would use to communicate with others. But he chose not to do so with his mother. She was, after all, unprepared.

So, he nudged her in thanksgiving and farewell, and her eyes saddened as she realised that they would meet no more. That his life lay elsewhere, that she could not follow. She would stay with her kind, would have other foals to console her loss and fulfil her motherhood. But her One-Horned-Foal – her One-Horn – would be away from her forever. Except in her memory….

A whinny of farewell, and One-Horn stepped back on his sturdy legs, raised and lowered his head in homage to his mother. His horn shone in the early morning sun through the leaves of the glade where he had been born.

Then he whirled in a flash and was off. First in a slow canter, then picking up speed he was gone with a rush of hooves into the distance. Only the leaves rustling behind gave a clue as to where he had been. His mother walked slowly away towards the others of the herd…...

CHAPTER 3

After: The Stuff of Legend

"Equus Unicornis", "The One-Horned Horse", as he came to be called when the world of Science came around to giving him a Latin name, was more than mere myth. Though born of natural parents, he none the less was not bound by the normal laws of nature. The crystals and their blue beam had seen to that…...

He had no real need of food as did other creatures. Though of solid flesh, yet his body would resist age and ageing, though none could know for how long.

He would be tireless as he roamed the world, yet he would have to fulfil an inner need to stay and observe the doings of Man and beast.

He would need only minimal rest, to be able to take time to reflect and understand all that was happening around him.

Being one of a kind and unique in his own species, he would not seek a mate. Far from being lonely, he would be happy in future centuries when the children laughed in the rain and when the crops were gathered in and there was dancing in the village. And when new life came into the world…

But he would be sad when old and tired life had to leave, when anger snarled and the sabre flashed, when death stalked the land and there was weeping in the corners and in the darkened houses behind drawn blinds.

For the crystals and their Blue Light had also given him Sentiment.

He was very, very careful about letting himself being seen. Except on the rarest of occasions, he never spoke to humans; he had learnt that they were not to be trusted, even the kindest or the poorest. And so, the legends about him began….and grew…

In Japan his shadow, with the horn to prove it, was seen in the perfumed garden of a Shinto shrine. He ran among the yaks of Mongolia and the reindeer of Lapland, as their herdsmen gaped. He was seen in the Caucasian tundra, and in the Piedmont valleys of Italy.

An Englishman spied him in Canterbury and had him included in a stained-glass window, he was put into an illuminated Bible at Monte Cassino, and the Arabs watched in wonder as he easily outpaced their fastest purebreds as they raced across the desert sands.

Neither did the heat of the Sahara nor the cold of the steppes hold any terror for him, and he easily covered wide stretches of open water in the tropics and in the polar seas. The Inuit (a) of the Arctic mistook him for the hornèd narwhal (b), saw him watching the great white bears as they caught the seals at their breathing-holes. And men of Science mistakenly identified dinosaur bones as being those of other members of his family....

The legends spoke of him as being immortal – which was probably false – as being un-capturable, except by a spotless virgin – which was probably true, – as being a bearer of good news, or even of bad news. All depended on the interpretation.

But whatever it may have been, the truth is that the One-Horn existed, unproved and seemingly unproveable. So many instances of fleet sightings around the globe could not be pure invention, as the excited *gaucho* of the Argentinian Pampas who claimed to have nearly caught him with his *bolas*, or the Mohawk who saw his shadow in the moonlight through the skin of his *wigwam*.

Finally, he was dismissed as myth, which probably suited him best, as he could then move about more freely.

The gift of Thought-Speech he carefully concealed, and so could capture and understand any of the idioms and thoughts of Man at will as he travelled. But he rarely Thought-Spoke to humans, and then only briefly. He was more at ease and spoke more and learned more from the animals. They feared him less, and he was, after all, one of their kind......

Yet the most useful – and strangest – gift he had received was that of near-invisibility. Should he be in a difficult situation where escape was impossible, or should he wish to approach humans or animals without being seen, he had merely to touch his horn to hard rock, and at once his solid body would become a faint blue haze, just barely visible. And so he was able to get in close to observe and not be seen, while life went on all around him, oblivious to his presence. Thought-Speech was possible even in such a state of haze, a definite advantage, and to return to his original state a mere touch of the horn-haze to another rock would set things normal again.

On his travels he had many occasions to use this magnificent gift, especially when approaching the young or the primitive. But he was caught out one day......

One may ask, why did he keep always on the move? and why shun the intimacy of Man? And why had the Light-beam chosen him above all others to give him its incredible gifts? And was his horn for good or for evil? Why? Why? Why?

So many questions, and so few answers. Let us therefore be patient. And maybe we will learn:

The Secret of the Unicorn.

Part 2

CHAPTER 4

Start

Life on Big-World-Earth had started because there had been water. This itself had come about through the improbable and fortuitous union of gases under electrical discharge, which, generalised, became droplets, then rain, lakes, rivers, seas, oceans, over billions of years.

It was in the estuary waters that the proteins, carbohydrates, amino-acids, salts...... all combined over untold generations and many failures and dead-ends, to produce the very simplest of one-celled living matter, the protozoa.

From then on there was no holding back. Many millions of years on, unicellular matter had combined and become infinitely more complex in the waters of Big-World-Earth. Reproduction, the demands of survival, crossings-over of the very first individuals, fixation of their species into immutable lines, all these combined to give an infinite variety of water-creatures – fish, snakes, scaly and smooth-skinned giants of the deep; and in the shallower waters, the smaller species, each of which had its own code of survival. Some gave birth to living young, many laid eggs to assure continuation.

Some fish had stiffer fins than others, and these helped them to drag themselves across the mud-flats and coastal mangroves for protection or to seek food elsewhere. Most returned to the water, but a tiny minority had air-sacs which adapted to the air above the water, and whose bodies in time became accustomed to the sun. Gradually these air-sacs developed into lungs; gills and fish-tails atrophied and became useless. Things of the water had become things of the land, able to find food, protect themselves, reproduce, continue the species.....and so began the slow and painful evolution into land-based animals. Some – most snakes and the varieties of crocodiles and alligators – laid eggs, but most gave birth to living young. And some land-based animals – newts, salamanders, toads, frogs – returned to their water-mother to reproduce.

Millions of years later, the bodies of these primitive pioneers had indeed changed radically. Most were no more of the water, but of the land. Their hard scales had evolved into primitive clasping appendages, aiding in propulsion, gathering food, protection...

But for three hundred million years the lizards ruled the Earth, evolving into unbelievable gigantism and variety. The biggest was a vegetarian of forty metres long, the smallest no bigger than a sparrow. The fiercest was an eight-metre high carnivorous giant, with many sub-species and genera among them. Some were in the marshes, some in the estuaries, some in the oceans. Some flew….but as yet there was no Man…..

It was around this time that the primitive horses evolved (a). And from this line came the only One-Horn ever to exist….

CHAPTER 5
Meteor

Eons passed slowly as only eons could, interminably, with few changes on the Earth. The lizard-kind covered practically all the land surface, and the waters were themselves filled with the uncountable variety of water-creatures, some breathing air through blow-holes in their heads, others through their gills. Each species fighting endlessly for survival.

Through the centuries the Unicorn moved around freely. He was fleet enough to escape all predators, dangers were few. He saw the clumsy leaf-eating dinosaurs wallow in their swamps and coastlands, saw certain groups move in herds and protect their young in the centre. He saw stragglers attacked and ripped apart by the flesh-eaters, saw their agonies and jerking deaths as more arrived for the feast, saw their bones picked clean when it was all over.

Sometimes he would try Thought-Speech with the lizard-kings. He saw them jerk their heads upwards as the thought-waves reached their brain, but they were dim-witted and unable to reply. He stopped trying.

The same thing happened at the water's edge, with even poorer results. So he finally gave up trying to communicate, and left them to their apparently meaningless lives.

The millions of years wore on, and life and the lizard-kings had filled most of the Earth. In the mysterious depths of the oceans even more wonders evolved and reproduced and died, their bodies slowly sinking into the watery depths even as the huge land masses cracked and drifted apart along the fault-lines of the Earth (a).

The Unicorn had crossed the tundra and steppes of the vast eastern

17

land mass of what would one day become Siberia, and gone over into the great plains of "North America". He then continued even further south into the river-deltas of the southern continent, when the unimaginable happened.

Suddenly the night sky became as day when the immense meteor entered the Earth's atmosphere. Moving at tremendous speed, its path was more direct than the Moon's had been so many eons ago, and it couldn't escape the insistent pull of gravity, nor the shield of Earth's atmosphere. Impact was certain.

Crackling and hissing as it entered the upper layers of the atmosphere, rock melted on its surface and broke into flaming pieces. Released gases burned away and followed them in a fiery tail as the meteor streaked across the sky, heading straight for the Earth.

The dinosaurs along the entry path of the meteor across the world looked up dumbly as the hissing and crackling of the fireball passed overhead and disappeared to the west. They could not then know it, but their reign would soon be over.

Far to the west, the Unicorn in the delta saw the steep angle of the streaking fireball pass over his head, and followed its descent as it fell to Earth beyond the horizon (b).

The shock of impact could be felt underfoot even where he was, half-a-continent away, and the boom of the explosion came plainly to his ears. Earth shuddered as her mass took the full brunt of the collision. Flames from the super-heated mass of the meteor and the heat generated by the force of the impact caused the nearby trees to burst into flames and explode. The fire spread rapidly, aided by the searing heat of the wind. Smoke in dense clouds and dust from the impact rose with the flames into the air, pushed along by the choking atmosphere.

Fires spread ever more rapidly as the superheated air caused the resin of the trees to bubble and boil, and soon the trees themselves were exploding and burning. The heat continued to rise into the upper air with the smoke and dust, the thickened dark clouds continued to expand. Soon the Unicorn from his distant refuge could see them extending outwards and rising ever higher. In the space of a year the clouds reached from horizon to horizon, and the forests continued to burn and burn uncontrollably.

Even the water in the delta did not offer full protection to the Unicorn. The fires advanced over the endless forests, right to the water's edge, and he had to retreat before its endless advance, fascinated by the destruction which seemed unstoppable.

The fires in the tropics continued to spread and burn for several years, fanned by the wind and carried along by its own heat. And the dust and smoke thickened and rose, and continued to spread even to the ever-frozen regions. And it was then that the Sun's rays found it impossible to give their life to Big World.

The Earth took a long time to cool under its thick coat of smoke and dust, and it was then that the Unicorn saw the full extent of the changes brought about by the fall of the meteor.

The first to die were the plants on the plains and around the water-courses, those which had survived the conflagration. The sunlight they needed for growth and seeding was gone, so they yellowed and wilted and rotted on their stalks, useless for food.

The huge leaf-eaters were the next to go. Unable to find enough vegetation to sustain their bulk, whole families of duck-billed dinosaurs died together, grouped around the eggs in their nests. The brontos and stegos and ankylos, and so many other species, grew ever thinner and wasted, and finally starved to death, victims of a catastrophe which they could neither understand nor control. Their world was gone. Forever.

The last of the lizard kingdom to go were the flesh-eaters. From the tiny chicken-sized hoppers to the immense iguanodons and tyrannos they died in the open plains and near the lakes, where they vainly tried to keep alive on the rotting corpses of the leaf-eaters. Then they too had to obey nature's law of no return.

The Unicorn – now "Uni" to us – saw all these terrible happenings as he travelled around the devastated Earth. From the plains and forests of what would one day be the "Americas" to the immensity of "Africa" and the steppes of "Mongolia", he came across the bodies of the lizards, already decomposed and beginning to be covered by thick dust and mud, in the same places where they had died, leaving only their skeletons to be found by future generations. Only the smaller ones had survived –but only just – and in the coming centuries they too would be no more.

Water-creatures fared little better than the lizard-kings, as the same effects in the aquatic food-chain had occurred. The death of the water-plants in the shallows also sounded the tocsin for the plant-eaters, followed by the flesh-eaters, and very few from those early days survived to prove the past to future Man (c).

CHAPTER 6

Restart

Paradoxically, it was the wholesale demise of the entire range of lizard-kings which gave a new chance to the animal world to take new directions. Gigantism had all but disappeared on land, except for the latecomers, the mammoths and rhinos and giant ostrich-like birds (a). In the oceans the blue whale became the largest living creature ever, followed by a whole series of smaller species.

On the land, and over millions of years, small lemur-like creatures in trees developed into the great apes on the one hand – gorillas, chimpanzees, orangutans – and into the bands of shuffling man-like creatures – the hominids – on the other. The Unicorn noted that both these developments took place in the warm humid valleys of East Africa, near the water-courses where gathering fruit was a relatively simple task (b).

Like the great apes, the hominids lived in clans, huddling together for protection from the dangers of the night, but unlike the other groups, one clan of hominids in particular began to develop in a way peculiar to itself.

Instead of bending forward to walk on their knuckles as did the apes, one member of this group had found that standing upright gave a farther view of the fruit-trees, even though this caused some problem of balance. It began with difficulty to walk upright, using its arms to reach upwards to gather fruit, instead of picking them up from off the ground. This was noticed by the others, and so imitation began, not without difficulty as unaccustomed muscles were called in to give service....

Little by little over the centuries their hips and leg-bones became firmer and straighter, and the hunched-over ape-like position had gone forever. All were now walking upright as a group, they could plan as a group, gather fruit and see further for newer and better fruit, as a group. Their brains had also developed with the effort, as had their hands with the opposing thumb, quite unlike the great apes.

The Unicorn drew near as a blue haze, and to his surprise he found them starting to formulate thought-words. "Water", "food", "good", "bad", "danger", "stone", "rest", all these became fixed concepts which all of the group seemed to recognize and accept. They grunted and squealed and huffed to make the sounds correspond to the ideas, and slowly began to link these ideas in chain form.

"Food good, stone danger, no eat", then "food eat, rest good". Uni caught these thoughts as they huddled together at night for warmth and protection against the great cats and the cold air. He marvelled at the flexibility of the way they were thinking, at how they were getting their ideas across...

It was after a sudden thunderstorm that the group found the bodies of a family of lemurs burnt alive in the bole of a tree which lightning had struck. The smell of burnt flesh was new to them, and a tentative nibble to it brought a grunt of surprise, then to a bigger bite, and soon the bodies of the lemurs were being torn apart by eager teeth as the new taste registered.

Thus, they discovered the importance of fire to cook their meat, to warm themselves in the chilly nights, and to keep the leopards and lions at a respectful distance beyond their thorn bushes. So they learned the use of this new element; but they could still not create fire at will, and were limited to keeping alight the one at their campsite, or moving only short distances away with glowing embers in a gourd to restart the fire.

One of the group was therefore appointed "Carer of the Fire", and it was to this member that the group came after a hunt with their little stone tools to char their meat before eating it. Fire thus became an important part of their lives, and to be "Carer of the Fire" was indeed an important post. But woe to him if the Fire were allowed to go out....

It was only when they had learned to create fire by striking sparks upon dried moss using flintstones that their first big problem was solved. The group had been severely limited in its movements through their need to return to the campsite nightly for protection and food, and the supply of available wood to keep the fire going was seriously diminishing.

In the meantime, their grasping of new thoughts and words to express them came through slowly to the Unicorn as he approached them, huddled around their little fires at night.

The words faltered at first, then took definite sounds: "me", "thing", "child", "make", "you", "female", "go", "come"; then, "fight", "want", "far", "fire", sometimes linking the words: "male want female want child want food eat rest good". And so it went, year after year......

This handling of ideas and sounds to make intelligible words gradually filtered into the council around the fire, and centered around their preoccupation of becoming more mobile, of even facing the necessity of migrating. They debated the problem:

"Here good food fire eat good rest good me here", said one.

"No no no wood end no fire no food no eat we die go go go," said another.

"Me make fire, we go, find food eat happy rest, go go go" said a third. The others looked on and grunted as the ideas came thick and fast.

And so, the first *pre-Homo Sapiens* came face to face with the problem of a group decision, a necessity which would be one of the cornerstones of society in future centuries, as Uni in haze-form came to see it. He also concluded that they were worried, but saw that they had one great consolation. They could carry their fire-stones, dried moss and wood would be plentiful elsewhere. They could make fire!

The grunting and squealing and huffings became more animated as the implications of their discussion sank in. The group was becoming confident enough to leave the security of their gorges near the river and move out. They were all descendants of the original group, and it had taken them thousands of years for clans to form, chieftains to be chosen, allegiances to be made. Besides, they were hunter-gatherers, not farmers, and more mouths to feed meant more food was necessary. Their ancestral lands could only support limited numbers, so migration seemed the only means to survival, even though it would mean facing the unknown. It was thus that they saw the problem...

So, the die was cast by common consent, and early one morning the big group broke up into separate clans, each led by its own chief, their only possessions the skins they wore, the little stone cutters and tools in their hands, their throwing-sticks and lances. Gone was the need to carry a fire-gourd...they would live off the land using their intelligence and their skill in making fire!

The females and children were in the centre of the walking circle of hominids, armed males ringed them, scouts were far to the front, guards to the sides and rear.

And so they migrated, over several thousands of years. Some went southwards, where their descendants would remain as the Bushmen of the Kalahari; some went westwards across the wet-lands of what would later become the Sahara, leaving their rock-paintings of hippo, elephant and crocodiles behind them to prove their passage (c). They continued north over the land-bridge joining Africa to Europa, and would become the Neanderthal, the Cro-Magnon, the ancestors of modern Man......

Still others went due north, across the land-bridges to the Near and Far East, into China, Mongolia, the peninsulas of the Asian sub-continent, and would evolve into Synanthropic Man...And so the migrations went on and on, and the hominids slowly evolved as their awareness of themselves and their abilities increased with the passing of the centuries.

Uni the Unicorn was free to come and go as he wished, and so would spend long periods near one or other of these groups. He would see how they learnt to master fire-making techniques. They learnt the art of polishing stones to make them sharper, to make tiny arrowheads from flint and animal bones, to master the bow and the lance, to brew poison from insect larvae and animal bile, to begin to bury their dead and wail over them. And they devised rites to conjure up the spirits of good fortune when a hunt was imminent, the group's *shaman* (d) dancing in the skin and horns of the intended prey as the hunters grunted in unison in a circle around the fire.

The Unicorn silently followed the shaman one day as he went deep into a grotto with his painting-sticks and bowls of coloured clay. Deeper and deeper along a sloping track under the mountain, following the Forbidden Path, lighting his way with the little oil-lamp held in front of him.

The shaman came to a smooth wall at the end of the path, and set the lamp on a rock. In its glimmer Uni could see the drawings of bison, antelope, lion, of armed hunters, pregnant females, repeated over and over on the smooth rock. Amazed at such revelations, he stepped closer to get a better view, forgetting that he was not in haze-form....

His hoof clinked against a rock and in a flash the shaman had whirled around and came face to face with him. His jaw dropped open in surprise, his eyes widened in the gleam of the little oil-lamp.

What you? came the thought from the shaman, grabbing the stone knife from his belt.

You no fear thought-spoke the Unicorn, stepping backwards. *Me One-Horn. Me no spirit. Me follow here. You man who?*

Me Oogog. What want you?

Me want see what you do.

Not able. Images on wall for good hunt, for make children. If you see, all finish. We die

Then me go. Me not want hurt.

Why you One-Horn? What mean? Where come from?

Me very very old, One-Horn from far sky. Me only One-Horn.

You Great Spirit? You give good hunt?

Me not Great Spirit. Me born too, long time. Me hope you good hunt. Me not come back.

He stepped backwards as he said this, whirled swiftly and was gone up the path leading to the grotto's entrance. Soon he was far from the little encampment of the band of hominids. To think.

The shaman sat trembling in front of the little oil-lamp, unable to believe what had happened. He had had a thought-conversation with a wondrous white horse. A horse with a horn on its forehead, like no other horse he had ever seen, even the wild ones. Had it been just a dream? He got up and looked in the dust. No, the hoofprints were still there, it had all been so real.

He looked at the portion of blank stone wall in front of him, and swiftly set to work with his pots and paint-stick. He had a job to do......

An hour later he stepped back to judge his work. *It good, very good*, he thought, as he put the finishing touch to the Unicorn's profile. The face seemed almost alive and the horn a good omen, as he touched it for the last time.

You not Great Spirit, you say, but we to have good hunt. Go you way, One-Horn, we be happy happy here.

Oogog the Cro-Magnon bowed to the image of the Unicorn and made his way slowly back up the grotto's path. He would not tell anyone of what had happened. Who would ever believe him? Let the future find the image......if it were lucky enough to find the Forbidden Path......

Chapter 7

Moriah

He'd followed the crazy-looking old man at a distance up the little hill to the uneven outcrop of rock on top, and now the oldster was trembling with emotion as he put down the pot with the glowing embers. He straightened up and looked around at the area around the rock: Nothing but spindly bushes and dry land. Far away the desert hills shimmered in the midday heat, and here and there the bleat of wild goats came faintly to him. He breathed more easily now as his body overcame the effort of the climb, and turned slowly to look behind him.

Just a few yards away stood waiting the young boy of ten, breathing hard under the large bundle of dried faggots tied together and balanced on his head. He stood waiting the oldster's order to throw it down, and did so gratefully when the nod came. It had been a long trek under the hot desert sun, almost a whole day's march with just water and dried dates to calm his thirst at the last well in the valley below. Now perhaps Papa would offer his sacrifice as he had intended. *"Yahweh will provide the lamb, my son"* he'd said, and Isaac had believed him. Never before had his father lied to him. Then maybe they could rest…...he was so tired.…

It had all begun so many years ago. The Unicorn had followed the fortunes of the various early hominids around Europa and Asia. He'd seen the groups increase and migrate, saw them fight for territory, hunt the fierce cave-bear in Europa and the mammoth in the Siberian wastes, steal wives from each other's' clans, develop worship-cults, cultivate the wild grasses and bring the first wild animals under control – wild sheep, goats, dogs, camels.…

He'd seen some groups become unable to adapt to new ways and disappear forever, leaving behind only their humble tombs and stone tools, as well as their impressive religious monuments scattered throughout Europa and elsewhere (a).

Yet these early hominids had evolved into *Homo Sapiens Sapiens – Man who knows himself* – settling in towns and cities, learning ever new things, waging war with ever newer weapons, learning awkwardly and violently what they were really meant to be – Masters of the World.

It was in Ur in Mesopotamia that the Unicorn saw the sacrifices of the first-born to the terrible bloodthirsty god Moloch. It was there too that he saw the first timid steps in transcribing sound and ideas – writing was being given birth, using wet clay tablets and wooden stylets, by the tribeswomen...

And it was from there too that he saw the departure of Abram and his little clan (b), disgusted at the endless child-sacrifices to the gods. The whole clan left – men, women, children, animals, – and headed west for the nomadic life of the Bedouin in the desert wastes of the Negeb.

Abram interested Uni. He was a restless thinker, a seeker of meaning and truth, and offered the usual animals from his flocks in sacrifice, as did so many others of his time. But one unforgettable night, when a strange light came from nowhere and seemed to envelope the sacrifices he had offered (c), Abram and his wife Sarah, though old and childless, were able to engender and bring into the world a little boy, whom Abram – though he now proudly called himself Abraham, in recognition of his new role as father – called Isaac, the "Child of the Promise". How they doted on the boy! From him would spring countless generations! (d).

But now everything seemed to have gone terribly wrong. Abraham seemed to have lost his zest for life. He sat in the shade of his tent for long days, just looking out into the desert. And sometimes he just sat under a nearby tree and did the same. The little boy always played nearby, and many times tears filled the old man's eyes as he watched his son's innocent play. Sarah stood by, looking at them, a worried look in her eyes.

Finally, Abraham broke the silence. *"Yahweh has ordered me to sacrifice our child"*, he explained to the horror-stricken Sarah, *"on Moriah, where the pagans sacrifice, and I must obey. Tomorrow you will bid him farewell for ever".*

"Have you gone mad?" she whispered hoarsely. *"You made us all leave Ur because the infant sacrifices disgusted you (e), and now you yourself are going to sacrifice our only child? I don't believe it was Yahweh at all who spoke to you. It must have been the Evil One himself!"*

"No, it was Yahweh, I tell you, woman. I must do as he has said, and we must have faith that all will be well. Trust Yahweh". He paused, then stood up. *"We leave at dawn,"* he said.

Sarah was not to be seen as they left before sun-up for far-off Moriah with the boy seated on the donkey led by a servant, but Abraham knew that she was weeping inside the drawn folds of her tent door. The prospect of a long trip excited the boy, and he kept up an endless chatter as they plodded along the dusty desert path for three days, pointing out the rodents on their mounds, the little birds and coloured turtles of the desert. The Unicorn was well able to conceal himself among the dunes and changing desert colours and rock forms, so had no trouble following the little group.

They'd camped at the last watering-hole before Moriah when Isaac blurted out, *"Father, we have everything here for the sacrifice: the wood, the fire, the knife. But I see no lamb for the offering!"*

"Yahweh Himself will provide the lamb, my son" was the reply, and the answer seemed to satisfy the child's curiosity. They left the servant and donkey in the valley and began the long climb upwards together.

So, they had at last arrived at Moriah, the very place which symbolised the disgust Abraham felt for the pagans who sacrificed there. And now he was going to be even lower than they!

"Yahweh, I trust!", he prayed.

He collected the faggots the boy had thrown down, arranged them into a rectangular altar-form, and before Isaac could realise it, he had been bound and gagged and laid across them. Abraham seized his knife…

Crouched behind the sparse desert shrubbery, the Unicorn was horrified. How could such a monstrous act be tolerated? He gathered himself to spring.…

And then the bleat came from a nearby bush, the bleat of a goat in trouble. Abraham and the Unicorn both heard it at the same time, and saw a ram struggling to get free from under the bush where he'd been resting. It had been startled by Abraham's sudden movements and had caught its horns in the branches as it had tried to escape!

In a flash Abraham was upon it and had bound its legs together. *"Yahweh has kept his promise! Great is his name!"* he cried.

He returned to his child still bound and gagged, wide-eyed at the turn events had taken, and tenderly untied him. He held the boy against his chest and was weeping, sobbing uncontrollably for joy and relief.

"Forgive me, my son, but Yahweh must always be first, even before my dearest hope. And look! He has indeed provided!" But the weeping child did not reply.

Abraham put the ram on the altar and seized the knife again. It flashed down…...(f).

Uni the Unicorn pondered on these strange events as he watched them move slowly away on the return journey. How could he understand man? What would Isaac's feelings towards his father be from this day onward? How would Sarah feel on seeing them both return? And who was this "Yahweh" anyway? He looked backwards toward the hill where the smoke from the sacrificial fire was still rising, and curled up under a palm tree to think it over…...

CHAPTER 8

The Chosen

He'd been gone for long centuries. He'd seen the immense wastes of the Mongolian highlands, where the long-haired yaks were herded by the upland farmers for their flesh and milk and for their warm pelts. Sometimes the yaks slept in the same huts with their owners, but mainly braved the intense cold and sheeting snow-storms in the open. And he'd seen the Mongols tame the little wild horses and learn to ride. In later centuries they'd become an armed force to contend with (a).

The slant-eyed light-skinned peoples of the coastal peninsulas fascinated the Unicorn. They fought often, mostly over land or females, but none could equal their patience as workers in the fields of water, where they grew the wild rice. They were great travellers, and took their culture, art and language to the far-off islands of the East, where the sun rose every morning from the sea (b).

He returned to the land where Abraham had settled, and then travelled to the great continent south of it. There he saw the kingdoms of Ethiopia and Meroe, and even farther to the west, to the great expanses, where the black folk were as warlike as those of lighter skins. They raided for slaves as did the peoples of other parts of the world, valuing highly great quantities of gold, their rulers' bodies being fairly weighed down with the yellow metal in their ceremonies. In their forests he saw strange powerful beasts with long defensive tusks, for the most part gentle unless provoked. And there were the big cats…and huge running birds…and scaly water-lizards, much smaller than the dinosaurs of the earliest days, but still dangerous….

The Pyramid-People near the Eastern River (c) interested him most. They built huge monuments to honour their god-kings, none being more impressive than the pyramids. Planned by master mathematicians to the nearest centimetre, the sides of these enormous square structures rose by inclining planes high into the sky, ending in a point, tombs for the mummified god-kings. In each of them were elaborate tunnels and chambers, dead-ends and traps, so as to conceal the real emplacement of the god's tomb. He was buried with his favourite wives and courtesans, his horses, weapons and chariots, sometimes boats, with food and drink for the after-life.

But the grave-robbers saw through all these ruses, and many tombs were desecrated even before the cement had well dried. In many tombs the after-life of the god-king was seriously compromised, as his provisions were also stolen and dispersed to the four winds, not to speak of his jewellery guaranteeing after-death happiness.

The problem of the after-life preoccupied the Unicorn somewhat. He had seen death in many forms over the endless centuries – the mass-death of the dinosaurs, the battles for land and females among the hominids, the death of the helpless and weak, be they man or animal, the death of the strong. But what did it all mean? If man could have come as far as this point of building these impossible monuments in the hope of after-life, could there be in fact an after-life?

Uni suddenly felt frustrated. He tried to imagine how he would be at his death. After all, he was born millions of years ago, yet was as strong and alive as the day he was born and claimed by the Blue Light. And in fact, what had happened to it? He wondered, yet finally concluded that he had no real idea of the meaning of his own life, so how could he have an idea of death? He shook his head and gazed at the pyramid-builders. Did they have the answer?

The Unicorn found that these monuments were not built through love of the god-king, but through the coercion of slavery. Literally thousands of slaves were in the quarries cutting the immense blocks of stone, hundreds more hauling them across the sands on rollers and up inclined planes, all driven by men with whips and fire-brands. Deaths were common. A simple grave at the road-side was hastily scraped out, the dead bundled in, and on rolled the huge blocks amid the shouts of men and the crack of whips and the stink of burnt flesh.

"M'ses! M'ses!". The sound was coming through clearly now, from the tired minds of the slaves in the cold of the desert night around the fires. Uni's thought-speech caught the sound again and again as the men mumbled among themselves....

"...M'ses...the one found in the basket among the river-reeds..."

"...a slave like us, fled into the desert after killing a man..."

"...came back with a message, from a god who said he is YHWH....Yahweh...He-Who-Is..."

Yahweh again, thought the Unicorn, but who is he? The mystery was deepening...

"...said that the god-king must let the slaves go...to their own country..."

"...the god-king refused; no slaves must leave here..."

"...M'ses said we must be ready to leave...tonight..."

"...that each family must sacrifice and eat a lamb..."

That night Uni saw the amazing sight of thousands of slaves, men, women and children, gathering their meager belongings and assembling in excited groups after the ritual meal, while around them their masters urged them on to leave, weeping all the while and showing the lifeless bodies of their children and young animals, wiped out by some mysterious illness.

The crowd parted to let a tall man through. Stern and unsmiling, staff in hand, his very presence commanded respect and silence. He addressed the crowd:

"My brothers, the hand of Yahweh has been heavy upon our masters, as he had promised. Great is his Name! They have lost their first-born and are begging us to go, willing us to go, to leave this land of slavery behind. So be it! We leave then, a free people once again, and we return to the land of our ancestors. Such is the will of Yahweh!"

"M'ses! M'ses!" chanted the crowd, then more strongly, then with a roar. *"Mo-ses! Mo-ses! Mo-ses! Lead us to the Land of Promise! To freedom! Great is the Name of Yahweh! Great is his Name!"*

"Let us leave this land for ever, my brothers! Let no one look back! Yahweh will be our guide! Onward!!!"

He flourished his staff, and the crowd moved away to the east and into the desert. They would wander there for many years before coming to their land, the land of milk and honey promised in the ancient Alliance between Abraham and Yahweh in that unforgettable night so many years ago, in favour of his descendants, the Chosen Ones.

The Unicorn followed the Chosen People in their desert wanderings, always from a discreet distance. He saw them escape the god-king's soldiers sent to herd them back, saw them march by day following the clouds from the east, and at night by the light of the erupting volcano to the far west, hundreds of leagues away (d). Saw them collect the dried resin of the gum tree and the little quails for food, saw them make the Golden Calf and dance around it, saw them condemned by Moses as he came down from Mount Sinaï with the Tablets of the Law in his arms (e).

He saw them fight and drive off the pagan tribes in their march to the north, and finally saw them enter the Promised Land under Joshua their general (f).

Moses had died some years back, and had been buried on a mountain-top overlooking the Land of Promise. No one would ever find his final resting-place, no one would ever know where it was. Except the Unicorn – and he wasn't telling!

CHAPTER 9
Land of Wisdom

"Heya, Bap!, Heya, Rama!, Heya, Vishnu!, Heya, Shiva!". The clinking of the little thumb-cymbals and the shuffling feet of the chanting crowd came clearly to the Unicorn as he watched the curious dance of the Hindus. Back and forth, sway then three steps ahead, then two backwards. *"Heya, Bap!, Heya, Rama!".* Clink, clink, shuffle, sway, shuffle. *"Heya, Vishnu!, Heya, Shiva!"* Clink, clink, shuffle, shuffle, sway, clink. The boom of the metallic drums drowned out any opposing sounds.

And so it went on as he watched from the hillock overlooking the temple. This was a joyous occasion, giving honour to their gods carried on platforms held at shoulder-height and decorated with precious metals and jewels. It was coming to an end today, and would end with a feast of pork and chicken. These adorers of the Cow never sacrificed one of their gods for mere human feasting, but other beasts had a hard time…

Uni had been in India for long years. He had left the Promised Land far behind as the Chosen People began to organise their society based on the cult of Yahweh, their one God.

But here in far-off India things were different. There were gods enough and to spare, each with its myths, rites, priests and ceremonies. This was a land of colour and movement, with great wealth among the upper castes of the Brahmans, Vaishya, and others, and rank poverty among the lowest ones, the Harijans, the cleaners of public conveniences. A land of contrasts where the joy of a feast on one day would give way to a public cremation on the next. Uni saw with horror the rite of *suttee*, when a widow would immolate herself on the funeral pyre of her defunct husband.

And this was also a land of great fanaticism, as on the feast of Jaggernath, when devotees of the god risked themselves by running between the wheels of his huge platform as it was hauled through the narrow streets. Once Uni saw several crushed when they misjudged the speed and distance of the procession. He turned away from the screams and the sight of the mangled bodies……

Nevertheless, this was a cultured people. The myths of their gods were faithfully committed to Sanskrit, and in their Observatories the scientists of the day were able to prove the theories of helio-centrism and of gravity, centuries before Copernicus and Newton. They had discovered the value of the zero and of π, but....

But such knowledge was too dangerous to be taught openly, and so it was limited exclusively to the priestly class. It never became democratic, as it were, and as no great thinker ever emerged to promote and justify its universal application to everyday life, India and its knowledge turned in upon itself and stagnated.

And yet the Unicorn preferred these people with their many gods to the peoples where few gods were worshipped. They seemed more vital, and so his interests remained in India, rather than on the plains of Mongolia or the coastal countries to the east. India posed no question of Yahweh, the problem of whose existence he had not yet solved. But travel he must, and so to the north he went.

He was alone in the northern mountains of China when he saw the comet's light. It was coming in from the east and going west, moving slowly as comets do, and at times could be seen in broad daylight. But was it a comet?

The Unicorn was intrigued. Throughout his long life he had seen many comets, watched as the long tails behind the glowing mass came nearer and nearer to the Earth and then recede into the trackless distances of space. But this one seemed different. It seemed to beckon to him, almost as if he were being invited to follow its motion, which intrigued him even more. And so, for the first time in his long life, he began the journey to the west, not quite knowing what could be the meaning of it all. Would the comet suddenly disappear? Would it fall to Earth as the catastrophic meteor had done? Perplexed, he kept steadily on. Westwards.

CHAPTER 10
"He-Who-Is"

It was in the eastern desert of the Promised Land, long occupied by the tribes of the Chosen People, on the routes of the Nabatean desert-traders, that he first saw the caravan. But these were no traders, nor mere voyagers. A dozen armed men on swift desert horses escorted three majestic camels with their richly-apparelled riders. Following them were sturdy mules bearing heavy loads on their backs, linked together in single file and led by servants on their mounts. Two of the strange riders on camels were light-skinned and spoke in Aramaic, the ancient language of Abraham. The third was darker of colour and spoke in Sanskrit, the language of the learnèd in the Land of Wisdom. The thought-speech of the Unicorn caught much of their conversation, but he remained intrigued as they conversed among themselves and with their escort and servants. Who were these people, and where were they from? Above all, where were they going, and why?

That night Uni drew quietly near to the animals' enclosure while the men slept, and engaged the resting beasts of burden in thought-speech.

Hail to you all, brothers! I am the One-Horn, but do not fear, I seek only information. I mean no harm.

The animals turned in surprise to face the Unicorn, seeing one like them, but so different....and able to connect his thoughts to theirs. The Unicorn paused and let himself be examined and accepted. He went on.

I have been following the light above for many moons, and I have seen your caravan going in the same direction, and that you are not from here. Where are you from, and where are you going?

We are from Ur, from the Chaldean people, thought-spoke one of the three camels, *and two of our masters are Watchers of the Sky. They too have seen the light, and I heard them say that it was a sign that a king had been born. So they have decided to follow the light to go and honour him*.

And the third master, the dark-skinned one....?

He is from India, the Land of Wisdom, and he too is a Watcher of the Sky. He came to Ur following the light also, and so the three have travelled together.

But the king who has been born, who is he supposed to be?

According to the wise men of the Chosen, he is to be the Promised One, the Messiah, the Saviour of all peoples, of all creation, sent by Yahweh, the very image of Yahweh himself.

How strange! – thought-spoke the Unicorn. *Many centuries ago – for I have lived longer than you – I have heard the name "Yahweh", but as to its meaning…. Have you any idea?*

According to what I have understood, One-Horn, broke in one of the horses, *he is the great and only God Himself, the Creator of all. "Yahweh" in the language of the Chosen means "I-Am-Who-Am". My master in Ur believed in Yahweh, and he always spoke of Him as the One True God*.

The Unicorn paused in deep thought. He continued. *That would mean that all the hundreds of gods I have seen in so many places, Isis and Horus of the Pyramid-Builders, Dofini and Yi of the dark people of Africa, Shiva and Vishnu of India, Moloch and the Baals of Babylonia, all these are mere myth? Just substitutes for the One True God? Can this really be true?*

It seems that way, friend One-Horn, replied one of the other camels.

I will follow you at a distance then, and will see where the Watchers will go. This mystery is indeed too great!

So, for three more weeks the caravan wended its way westwards, passing near the Great Salt Sea, then climbed gradually through the low-lying hills, resting in the oasis of Jericho before the final climb to Jerusalem. Once there, the light in the sky seemed to grow dimmer, so the Watchers went into the city to ask about the king (a).

The Unicorn kept at a discreet distance, and only the camels and horses in the caravan knew about his presence. Finally, the Watchers returned, and as they remounted and set off for the south, the comet's light returned, more brightly than before.

They reached Bethlehem in the afternoon, and there the light went out definitely. They found the little family in a humble lodging, father, mother and the newly-born. The Watchers of the Sky dismounted and prostrated themselves before the bemused parents. The newly-born seemed to enjoy it all hugely, and chuckled to himself as the Watchers returned to their pack animals and came back with their fabulous gifts. They lingered awhile to explain to the child's parents who they were, and in the early morning took a different road to return to their own countries. One never knows what the jealousy of the monarch in Jerusalem might do!

The Unicorn touched his horn to a rock, and at once became a faint shimmering blue haze, so as not to frighten the child's parents. The haze came to the cradle where the child lay.

You are welcome, One-Horn, said the Child in thought-speech, and held out his little arms to the haze near the cradle. Uni felt a thrill run through his whole being at the touch.

You...you can speak to me?, replied the Unicorn in amazement.

Yes, and thank you for coming so far to visit me. You are indeed welcome, but I know that you will soon be gone again, he seemed to say with regret.

Little child, please tell me, where have you come from, and why?

I am from the very Being of Yahweh, the One True God. I have come to fulfil the promises of the prophets of the Chosen, now called "Hebrews", to reveal Yahweh as Love, and to save mankind.

But if you are from the very Being of Yahweh, that means......

Yes, that I myself am Yahweh. "I-Am-Who-Am", the Messiah, and there is no other.

The blue haze bowed down in adoration before the Child, before "He-Who-Is", and once again felt the thrill of His touch through the haze.

Go in peace, One-Horn, said the Child, and withdrawing its arms into the cradle, at once fell asleep. He'd only recently been born, and little babies get tired so easily....

The blue haze drifted outside, unseen by either parent, then once again became the Unicorn as its horn touched the rock. Uni took some time to realise what had happened, then chose the mountain paths leading away from Bethlehem, and so made his way into the stillness of the desert. He had some serious thinking to do.

Part 3

CHAPTER 11
Rubbish Dump

It was some short years later, nearing midday, and the roasting sun seemed to have summed up special reserves of its heat for this pre-Shabbat Friday in Jerusalem. The Unicorn had come a long way that day, pulled along by some inner foreboding that he himself was unable to explain. He could not recall having been really afraid all during his long life, but today seemed totally different to any other he had ever lived through. It was not just fear that seemed to well up in his chest, but a sense of impending weighty doom that blocked out all other thoughts as he drew near to the City of the Chosen People on the hill. He recalled that Abraham had been here, on Moriah, so many centuries ago....

Even before he reached the outer walls the clamour of the crowds came clearly to him. But this was no ordinary clamour, he noticed as he drew nearer, these were the shouts of people who seemed to have lost all sense of humanity. They were shouting all at once, baying as one, but Uni was able to pick out some of the words screamed above the general outcry as he edged through the city gate, in blue-haze form.

"....him! Blasphemer! Blasphemer! Son of God indeed! Messiah indeed!"

"...rid of him! Trickster! To the cross! To the cross! To the cross!"....

"...sphemer! Crucify! Crucify him! Crucify him! Him!"

These last few words seemed to catch the crowd's fancy, and soon became a catchphrase scanded in unison with chilling regularity.

"Him! Him! Crucify him! ... Him! Him! Crucify him!"

At a safe distance from the edge of the mob, Uni was able to see and hear most of the proceedings, carried out at the forefront of the huge fortress, at the side of the Temple esplanade. He gathered that it was some sort of trial, but it seemed to be ending now.

On a raised dais was seated a stern man in the customary red military toga of the Romans, whom Uni took to be the Governor of the City. At his side a slave was presenting an ewer of water, into which the Governor dipped his hands briefly, drying them afterwards on a towel.

"I see no fault in this man!", he shouted to the people and their chiefs. *"Take him yourselves then, and crucify him!"*. He seemed angry with himself.

"Let his blood be upon us and upon the heads of our children!", bayed the frenzied crowd. *"Him! Him! Crucify him!"*

To the governor's right stood the object of their attention, a tall man standing weakly with a red cape over his shoulders, a matted crown of common hillside thorns covering the whole head. He seemed to have been cruelly beaten by two soldiers, both of whom now stood behind him with the weighted leather-thonged whips still in their hands, impassible, ready to begin again if ordered to do so. Blood oozed down his forehead and through his hair, dripping from his bleeding body onto the dais, and Uni wondered how he could still stand after the terrible whipping he had received.

Yet the man still seemed to be master of the situation – he was looking at the crowd now, not with fear nor anger, but with what seemed to be compassion.

Then in a sudden surge of memory, the Unicorn rolled back the years and saw again the smiling newly-born baby in his cot in Bethlehem. Yes, of course! This man and the baby were the same….

And now the beaten man on the dais was again looking straight at him, at the blue-haze at the crowd's edge. The Unicorn knew that he had been recognised, that he was being welcomed again…

The following hour became utter hell for the Unicorn. He saw the tortured man bear the heavy cross-beam brought by the soldiers, saw him labour under its weight on his bloodied shoulders, saw him fall among the mocking crowd under the effect of the day's heat and his utter exhaustion, once, twice, three times, bruising his knees on the rough paving-stones of the streets of Jerusalem. He saw him pulled roughly to his feet again and slapped by the soldiery to urge him on, saw him speak briefly to a group of lamenting women, and for a longer moment to a beautiful middle-aged woman at the very inside of the pressing crowd.

Uni recognised this woman. She was the mother of the baby, and the man was gesturing upwards. The Unicorn caught his words faintly, something about *"….my Father's business…"* to his distraught mother, before being roughly pushed along by the soldiers.

The mob passed through the city gates and continued its chanting *"Him! Him! Crucify him!"* until the local rubbish-dump was reached on the outside of the walls. Here there were thrown the daily refuse from the city's homes, the rotten fruit and junk from the nearby market-place, all at the base of an oddly-shaped rock on the slight rise of earth, roughly resembling a skull.

On this little hillock were dressed several upright permanent crucifixion poles, each with its notch at the top for cross-beams to be fitted into. Such executions seemed to be common enough, concluded the Unicorn, when he had understood their horrible purpose.

The crowd stood back and looked on fascinated as the man was stripped naked and roughly thrown to the ground on his back. The soldiers pulled his arms outwards to the beam's extremities. One produced a hammer and two round-headed nails, sought the spot of entry on the wrist, and with a loud "Hanh!" drove the nail with one fierce blow through the wrist and into the beam beneath.

The man screamed, an animal scream, as the searing pain reached his brain, as the sharp point cut through nerves, tendon, flesh, and again and again as the second wrist was immobilised in its turn. He lay panting in agony looking upwards, his chest heaving in shock. The soldiers tied his underarms to the beam, then straightened up and lifted it with the groaning man attached to it. They pulled him backwards and with little effort lifted the beam and fitted it into the notch on the crucifixion pole.

Another then produced a longer nail, and while his companion held the man's feet firmly against the pole, with another loud "Hanh!" drove the nail through both feet, fixing them securely there. The man screamed again in his agony as his nude body slumped forward under its own weight, suspended by the nails through his wrists and the ropes under his arms.

At the space behind his head the soldiers nailed another thin board. Uni saw the lettering on it without understanding. It read "I.N.R.I." (a). But Uni hadn't been to school....

So, this was what he had come to, the Child of Bethlehem, who had claimed to have come from "Yahweh" himself. What had he done to deserve such a cruel and humiliating end? Had no one dared to defend him, to speak out for him? Who had been his lawyers in the trial? And in that little group of two women and a young man, looking on from nearby, Uni recognised his mother again. But the others? Had he no friends at all? He wondered....

Two other men had also been crucified with him, one on either side, and Uni heard people murmur that these were zealots, guerrillas for the cause of the Chosen People against the Roman occupation, professional assassins who had been caught and recognised. Uni was too far away from there to hear what they were saying to him, as the crowd was even more dense by now, but it was clear that some sort of conversation was going on among the three men.

Then the man pushed up on his nailed feet and called out in a strong voice *"My God, my God, why have you abandoned me?"*, and slumped forward again, his force spent. It was clear that he could only breathe in and out by pushing upwards on the nail. He was a big man....and weighty.

The mob was more interested in him than in the two other condemned men. Uni could hear their mocking remarks.

"He said that God was his Father. If that is so, then why doesn't God come down to save him? Or even Elijah the prophet? Ha-ha-ha! What a clown!"

"He saved others, now let him save himself! Come down now if you can, o king of the Jews!"

They were having great fun at seeing a fellow human suffer so atrociously, pointing at his pitiful efforts to breathe normally, his chest filled with unexpelled air by the weight of his body.

The man turned his head and said something to his mother and the young man, but the Unicorn could not catch what he had said, just the nod of consent of them both to his words. The young man put his arm around the shoulders of the mother protectively and drew her to one side (b).

Drawn by the scent of blood, the flies from the rubbish dump and the heaps of animal entrails and excreta had gathered upon the wounds and contusions of the crucified man. They were there in their thousands, on his head and in his eyes, on the pierced wrists and feet, on the bruised shoulders, on the knees which had taken the full brunt of the falls on the uneven stones of his agonising journey to the rubbish-dump. They buzzed and hummed as they sucked in the droplets of blood and salty sweat welling up from the tortured body, and with their piercing tongues they opened up new wounds and set to with gusto on their unprotected meal. Each movement of the man to breathe sent some flying away in alarm, but they returned at once to resume where they had left off, and finally didn't even bother to fly off as his movements became weaker….and they fed and sucked on and on….

The Unicorn calculated that it had been just over two hours since the man had been crucified. He had sweated profusely under the afternoon sun and with his efforts to breathe and the occasional spasms of trembling and pain which shook his frame. The blood had dried on his forearms and wrists and feet, so that even the swarms of flies were discouraged at not finding as much liquid food as before. His panting and breathing became ever weaker, and eventually he mumbled a word which Uni caught clearly.

"…. *thirsty!*"

Clearly, he was dying, his forces completely spent. A soldier pushed a wet sponge against his lips, and this seemed to give him new strength. He pushed up once again on his nailed feet, seemingly preparing to say something.

Even though the sun was still shining, Uni noticed that the afternoon was less warm than before. In fact, it was even growing chilly. He looked upwards, and saw dark clouds beginning to cover the sun's disc. Not just one little cloud, but many, and they seemed to be extending further and further in the sky, darker and darker. It was still an hour or so to sunset, Uni thought, and yet the sunlight seemed to have lost all its force. At *this* time of the year? he wondered……

The soldiers and people also looked up, saw the dark clouds covering the sun, felt the sudden chill of the unusual afternoon, drew their coats around them. Little by little, in groups of two or three, and even singly, they began leaving the rubbish dump. Their afternoon's entertainment was coming to an end, and they had their families to think about. And a warm evening meal….

Suddenly the crucified man pushed himself upwards, breathed in deeply, gathered his strength again, and cried out in a loud voice which Uni and the crowd could all plainly hear,

"*Father, I put my soul into your hands!*"

Then he gave a heaving sigh, a final shudder, and slumped forward, lifeless. His head fell to one side, the whole body went limp and hung down on the cross, still held firmly by the nails and ropes. He had gone to the one he had called "Father". It was all over.

But no. Flash after flash of lightning streaked between the thickened clouds, crash after crash of thunder pealed from horizon to horizon, their angry rumbling causing all to look upwards, surprised at the vehemence of the phenomenon, expecting a heavy downpour. Uni saw dismay and fear on the faces of many (c).

But no rain came, and the main bulk of the crowd drifted away as the lightning and thunder gradually came to an end, leaving just a few groups of people, the guards, and the mother of the dead crucified man and her little group. The Unicorn was able to draw nearer, and saw that she had been weeping, but was still upright, the young man standing protectively at her side. Evidently a woman of unusually strong character, thought the Unicorn.

They were still there about an hour later, when another group arrived, led by a white-haired man, accompanied by an important-looking soldier. He went to the cross of the dead man, looked up into his face, then put the point of his lance against the man's chest, and pushed upwards between the rib-spaces. The spear went in easily, into the very heart. Thick blood and a clear liquid flowed from the wound when he pulled it out, and oozed down the side of the pale body (d).

The soldier grunted on seeing this, and muttered *"He's dead all right! I'll report this to Pilate"*. Then he said to the white-haired man and his friends *"Take him down, you people, and bury him as you wish!"*, and to the guards he barked, *"All right men! Finish them off, and get on with it!"*. He was accustomed to command and be obeyed. He left.

The soldiers advanced and broke the shins of the two crucified zealots, making them unable to push upwards to breathe. They died screaming and gasping for air, asphyxiated, in under three minutes. Their guerrilla days were over. The other clusters of sympathisers moved forward....

The group around the dead man's mother gathered around his cross, seemingly uncertain about what to do next. But the white-haired man took charge, and he and his men rocked the whole cross slowly, back and forth until they were able to lift it, dead body and all, out of the hole and lay it gently upon the ground. They covered his mid-section with a discreet cloth.

The mother bent down and kissed the brow and cheek of her dead son. From a few yards away the Unicorn saw how deeply she herself was heart-broken and suffering, but it seemed to him that she was still under the shock of having witnessed this most terrible of executions. She was not weeping now. Weeping would come later......

They removed the inscription board from the cross, then the crown of thorns, and with much twisting and pulling with the tools they had brought along, they were finally able to pull out the nails deeply imbedded into the wood. Then the white-haired man spoke to the mother.

"Miriam", he said softly, *"I know that you are sorrowing deeply. But we have little time, my dear. The Shabbat is about to begin, we have no time to wash the body of your son, and to prepare a tomb now is out of the question. Would you accept the tomb that I have prepared for myself for the day of my own burial, to lay his body? It is but a few paces from here, in the little cemetery recently allocated by the Sanhedrin. We can perform the correct rites after the Shabbat".* He waited expectantly.

Then Miriam the mother spoke for the first time, the voice of a mature woman, soft and musical and firm. Just a few words, but that was enough for Uni to judge her delicacy.

"Thank you, Joseph. Yes, I do accept. You are very kind".

In the nearby tomb they had placed a long linen sheet on the stone slab. Gently they lifted the body off the cross and put it on half the sheet, crossing the dead man's hands over his mid-section. Glancing through the tomb's opening, Uni saw Miriam cover the body completely with some sweet-smelling powders from the panniers the man Joseph had brought. The other half of the sheet was then brought down over the head and down to the feet, where it was tucked under the heels. The jaw was kept in place by a cloth band passed under the chin and tied on top of the head, and other cloths were then securely wound around the body, at intervals. Miriam kissed her son in his burial shroud a last time, and the mourners all left the tomb (e).

A large stone disc was there, ready to be rolled into a niche to block the entrance to the tomb. Heaving and pushing, the men rolled it down and wedged it tightly, and the little group went off slowly to begin their day of total rest. The Shabbat, sacred to the Chosen People, had begun, and this Shabbat had been declared particularly holy by the High Priest. The sun had already set and night was coming on.

Of all the executions that he had seen through the centuries – the burnings, the flayings, and the impalings included – the Unicorn considered this to have been one of the very worst. This had not been a judicial execution, it seemed to him. The Governor's words returned *"I see no fault in this man!"*, but he had then delivered him up to be crucified, through fear of popular reaction and ignorance of the religion of these people. So, whose was the fault then? he wondered.

It could not have been that of the baying crowd. Those people had been just mindless pawns, egged on by a few expert rabble-rousers. No, the fault would lay with their leaders, who had been speaking with the Governor. It was undoubtedly their fault, and this had been a religious murder performed by men fearful for their ancient Faith. This was his conclusion as he sadly left the City and touched a rock before heading for the hills in the far-off distance.

But whatever could have been the reason for the strange trial and death of this man, it was clear to Uni that his claims had been rejected by the majority of the Chosen People, and that the body in the tomb was there to prove it.

But had he really said that he was the "Son of God", that Yahweh was his "Father", that he was the Messiah? The Unicorn remembered the baby in the hay, and the little mother, in Bethlehem...What did this all mean?

CHAPTER 12
Rise and Fall

The Parthenon gleaming white on the magnificent hilltop site of the Acropolis, the Temple of Artemis with the hawkers wheedling sesterces and drachmae from awe-struck tourists, the Agora with its steady stream of intellectual giants whose thoughts would form the Western World – Aristotle, Plato, Democritus, Socrates among them, – the mathematicians – Archimedes, Euclid, Pythagoras, – the artists and playwrights and sculptors – Aeschylus, Sophocles, Homer, Phidias – all gone. The Temples of the gods deserted, weeds breaking up the immaculate marble slabs in the peristyle, wild cats and mangy dogs slinking in the shadows. Greece was no more.

Roma had fared no better. The persecutions of Nero, Decius, Diocletian, Marcus Aurelius, all these had ended, but the great *Urbs* was a shamble. The Cloister of the Vestals, the Baths of Caracalla, the Forum, Trajan's immense market-place, the Coliseum, the Circus Maximus, all had totally lost their aura of greatness or had been destroyed by the neglect of centuries or by the invading hordes. *Who would have believed that such a disaster could happen?* wondered the Unicorn.

Roma had seemed invincible to him in the first century after his visit to Jerusalem. Its tramping Legionaries seemed victorious everywhere as the Children of the She-Wolf built roads into conquered territories for their traders, armies and tax collectors to move about freely. All countries bordering the Mediterranean Sea were brought under the yoke of the Emperor and the *Pax Romana*. Northern Africa and Europa – even the large island on the west coast inhabited by blue-painted savages – as well as defunct Greece and turbulent Palestine, gave in to the Legions and paid their taxes grudgingly.

Palaces and luxurious villas rose in all the conquered territories, as well as huge public theatres and baths, while the Senate at Roma defined the Law and had it applied throughout the Empire.

Yet Roman ideals and a sense of high destiny gradually gave way to nepotism and sycophancy, moral decadence and widespread corruption, and its moral weakness, even far from Roma, became all too evident when the Governor of Palestine, Pilate, had tried to get rid of the uncomfortable "Jesus affair" by the hand-washing ceremony of moral cowardice (a).

And the Child, "He-Who-Is", had been crucified on the local rubbish heap just outside the city walls of Jerusalem. From a distance the Unicorn had seen the incredible torture, suffering and death of the Child on the Cross of a criminal (b).

But – so said his followers only three days after the crucifixion – "though the human body of "He-Who-Is" may have died, yet his Divinity could not, and his body has returned to life from the dead. He is resurrected and lives. We have seen, touched and eaten with him!".

All this gave great matter for thought to the Unicorn.

A few short years later the Temple in Jerusalem was destroyed by the Legions of Titus, the Chosen People dispersed. Some 900 never-say-die zealots holed up near the Dead Sea on a mountain-top fortress, but all eventually committed mass suicide to avoid capture and enslavement (c).

The slow decline and fall of Imperial Roma were agonising, through a succession of brutal and inept Emperors, corrupt administrators, and continuing moral decadence. At one time there were more slaves in Roma than freemen, most of whom frittered away their existence with the "food and games" provided by the Emperors so as to maintain themselves in power. Roma was found wanting….

By the end of the fourth century "after Bethlehem", Roma had followed the inevitable down-ward path of the preceding great empires…. of the god-kings of the Pyramids, of Alexander the Greek, of the Assyrians. Revolts in conquered territories were successful against the formerly invincible Legions, now mainly composed of slaves and poorly-trained dragooned barbarians. Roma itself had been invaded several times by barbarian hordes and almost destroyed.

Wandering among the broken columns of the temples and the Forum, Uni the Unicorn could only wonder at the momentous changes that had overcome Roma the Invincible. Then he remembered his encounter with the Traveller four centuries before…...

CHAPTER 13
The Traveller

The weary Traveller drank from the water-gourd at his side as he rested in the shade of the wayside tree. He closed his eyes. It was then that the voice came to him.

Fear not. Rest. I too am a traveller. Be calm, for I would speak with you.

He had not heard the voice with his ears, yet the words could not be clearer. He kept his eyes closed, lest the phenomenon should go away. He thought-spoke in reply: *Who is it who is speaking to me? what do you want?*

I seek information. I am the One-Horn of the tales of old. Please, who are you and where are you going, all alone in these dangerous mountains?

My name is Thomas, said the Traveller. *I was born of the Chosen People, and for three years a dozen of us had followed a young rabbi called Jesus of Nassara (a) who performed great signs and wonders. He taught us and all the people about Yahweh, whom he called "Abba", Father*.

This must be the Child of Bethlehem, thought the Unicorn to himself.

For this he was handed over by the Governor to the leaders of the Chosen People to be crucified, under their own blasphemy laws, and he died and was buried. I had at first seriously doubted when, three days afterwards, my companions said that they had seen and talked with him. To prove that he was not a spirit, he even ate fish before their very eyes!

But I could no longer doubt when he himself later appeared to me, and when I put my finger into the wounds of his hands and feet, and my hand into his side which the lance had pierced, I could no longer contain myself. I fell to my knees and I cried out "My Lord and my God!"

He covered his face as the memory of that day caused the tears to gush from beneath his closed eyelids (b).

He said that we must go and proclaim the Good News to all in the world, that God is Father of Love and wishes all men to love one another and to have eternal life. He paused.

So, we began in Jerusalem but were rejected. Some of us then went to Roma, others to the northern countries. I myself went to the black folk of Ethiopia. And now I have left and am on my way to the East, from where the Watchers of the Sky came. And there I will end my days.

Do not open your eyes, said the voice. *I will give you the gift of strength for your journey, and good health*.

The Unicorn touched the head of the Traveller briefly with his horn, and tiredness flowed from his body as he felt strength surge anew. And hope.

Fare you well, Thomas, may your work be fruitful. Now you may open your eyes when I am gone. The Unicorn whirled, and in a rush of wind was soon out of sight.

Thomas opened his eyes and could just make out the form of the Unicorn and its incredible horn before it was lost to sight. He could hardly believe that he had been in conversation with the fabled One-Horn. But his recovered strength was proof that it had been real....

And so, he turned once more to the East and strode bravely onwards. He would eventually reach India – the Land of Wisdom – and proclaim the Good News there, in years to come.

But in the meantime, he did something that he hadn't done since he was a boy....
He whistled......

CHAPTER 14

Community

Uni the Unicorn made his way to Roma shortly afterwards, and to his amazement as he wandered over the unkempt gardens and ruined temples of the ancient gods, he realized that a moral and spiritual force was emerging which would save and purify much of the past.

From what he was able to gather through his thought-speech, the Child's followers had started to carry his message to the very centre of the Empire, to Roma itself. They firmly believed and taught that he had indeed returned to life, and based all their faith and actions on this incredible fact – that "He-Who-Is" had died on the Cross – and had risen from the dead!

But the Community of followers – now calling themselves Christians – recruited adepts from the very poor and among the slaves, and had become a hunted people. They performed their cult of the Risen Christus – their Messiah – in their little hidden chapels deep underground in the public cemeteries. Now and then they were hunted out and slaughtered in the sand of the vast Colosseum, or set alight as torches to amuse the dinner-guests of the rich. Even their leader – Peter the Fisherman – was martyred by upside-down crucifixion on the side of the Vatican Hill.

Even so, gradually the news of a Risen Man slowly penetrated into the blasé hearts of the wealthy Roman patricians, and little by little they too began to show an interest in the teachings of the Community. A slow process, as all this time Roma was still steadily decaying morally, rotting from the head down. Anti-Christian persecutions continued until the early Fourth Century "after Bethlehem", ending only when the Emperor Constantine declared Christians to be worthy citizens and free to worship as they wished (a). And he founded the new imperial city in the East, called Constantinople (b), all the better to govern more efficiently the vast Empire.

Notwithstanding this, Roma continued to rot internally. Barbarians penetrated her walls, laws were unenforced and unenforceable, and to all intents and purposes the Invincible Empire had ended.

Free now to come into the open, and basing themselves on the teachings of the Child of Nassara, the Christian Communities organised themselves, and soon their courage in proclaiming the Message came to the notice of the civil lawmakers of Roma. Because of this, many of the latter in fact joined the Community, and so changes in Roman society began....

There was seen a marked drop in divorce, and those who practised concubinage saw themselves reduced to a minority. Abortion, though not a major cause for concern, became to be considered a crime against the infinite value of the human person, and was cause for excommunication from the Community, not to mention it being branded as murder under civil law. Exposure of infant girls upon the local dung-heaps, the right of fathers in pagan Roman society, and infanticide pure and simple of unwanted children, were stamped out by Christian compassion in action. Honesty in public office, and anti-corruption measures were encouraged. The aged and orphans were taken care of, and charity became a known Christian hallmark. New values began taking hold....

Upon observing these immense changes in Roman society, the Unicorn called to mind the child sacrifices to Moloch and the sacred prostitution in the pagan societies of the East. Indeed, the Christian Community – now called "Church" or "Ecclesia" – had become a moral force to be reckoned with.

From being the centre of the vanished Empire, Roma had in fact become the national centre of the Ecclesia. Its leaders began to be chosen from among the members of the Communities, and little by little the moral authority of these men began to be respected and followed even in the provinces, far from Roma itself. It was clear that the authority of these Fishermen – so called because the first Head of the Community had been one – was to play an important role in the day-to-day running of Ecclesia.

Slowly but surely the Unicorn saw Ecclesia advance. To the East, to Turkey and Greece, to the northern countries where the barbarians lived, to the Picts and Scots and to the wild blue-painted "Angles" of the great western island, to the northern coast of Africa, from Egypt to the Kabyle mountains of Tunisia and Algeria, she sent her missionaries with the Good News. The Message was being accepted in many regions, but in many the heralds of the Child of Nassara paid with their lives; for the courage of their convictions, and for their faith.

Dioceses and parishes were gradually set up in these new regions under leaders chosen from the various Communities, and from the ruins of the Empire in Europa and northern Africa and in the East the Christian Ecclesia began slowly to rise and to establish itself, following the Child's order to *go and teach all nations*(c). Its spiritual centre remained in Roma, where subsequent Fishermen had their headquarters. In the East of the former Empire lived another top representative of the People of the New Alliance, as the Community also called itself, before whom the Fisherman at Roma took priority. This was of course Constantinople, the city founded by the first great Christian Emperor.

And from Constantinople was to come many of the great problems of Ecclesia......

CHAPTER 15
Nestor

The first of these immense problems was Nestor, or Nestorius, as Latinised custom then decreed…and the problem was because of the Child of Bethlehem.

According to what Uni was able to gather from the conversations among the people of Ecclesia, the very nature of the Child had become a burning issue. Who was he in fact? Having survived two centuries of persecution by Imperial Roma, Ecclesia was now in danger of breaking apart by new doctrines. The most important of these was put forward by Arius of Egypt (a), who denied that the Child of Bethlehem was "He-Who-Is". It took two great Councils of Ecclesia (b) to clarify her official teaching and get it accepted. And then came along the second great problem, that of Nestor…...

He was a brilliant orator, head of the Ecclesia at Constantinople. He too created a serious division among the faithful by denying the title "Mother of God" to the Child's own Mother, thus implying that the Child himself was not "He-Who-Is".

Another Council of Ecclesia – by now understood and accepted to be the authority and arbiter in these delicate matters – condemned this teaching (c), and soon Nestor was sent packing into exile in north Africa, where he died some years later, reconciled with the Fisherman at Roma.

His followers fled into the desert wastes or to the great cities of the East, and for two hundred years the Unicorn watched the "Nestorians" as they organised themselves and sent their missionaries to spread their own version of the Good News, first into the cities around the ancient Ur of Abraham, then into India and finally deep into China. To the north they went to lands of the barbarians, and to Turkey and Egypt.

But it was the land to the south – Arabia – which interested the Unicorn most. He saw the Nestorian missionaries move slowly down into the desert wastes on mule and camel. They settled where there was water and human contact, mainly along the coasts. They built their little churches near the synagogues of the former Chosen People – the Hebrews – for in fact there were many of these who had settled there also, having fled to the south after the destruction of the Temple in Jerusalem, hundreds of years before. And there they continued to practise their ancient Faith – Judaism.

The Nestorians entered into theological conflict with the Hebrew leaders, the Rabbis, who were still awaiting the coming of the Messiah, while the Nestorians affirmed that he had indeed come, that he was Jesus, but that the same Jesus was merely human, not "He-Who-Is".

The bemused Unicorn saw with alarm the growing acrimony between these two communities, each with its own peculiar idea of "He-Who-Is". He saw the tensions build up, saw them choose the other side of the walkways when their paths crossed. He heard the wayside preachers of the ones denounce the "Christ-killers!", heard the Rabbis in return cry against the "cannibals who eat the flesh of the newly-born!". He saw the occasional riot, the occasional burning of synagogue or church, the occasional lynching…

And all this in a vast country of Bedouin and nomads who criss-crossed the land with their caravans of mules and camels. Nomads who were neither Hebrew nor Christian, nomads with their many gods demanding sacrifice, bearing spices, perfumes, embalming herbs – myrrh, frankincense, laudanum – for Egypt and the Mediterranean countries, on the backs of their patient "ships of the desert".

The Unicorn wondered – what did these nomads make of these two opposed communities? Could they make any sense of their quarrels at all?

CHAPTER 16
Messenger

The camel protested hoarsely as the rider hauled on the reins, but knelt gracefully as only camels do, front legs curled up first, followed by the hind. The rider slid off the hump-saddle in front of the low-slung mud-brick doorway and clapped his hands, gave the reins to the porter who emerged from the shadows, and stepped inside the open door.

The coolness of the building was in stark contrast to the desert heat outside, and Mahmoud drank gratefully from the large stone jar set in the corner, filled with water which became even cooler as the desert day warmed. A hooded man came in from the inner courtyard.

"*Salaam aleikum, Mahmoud*", said the Nestorian monk. "*Welcome to our humble home. You are back!*"

"*Aleikum salaam, Abuna Sergius*", replied the other, accepting the hand offered in greeting. "*Thank you for receiving me*". They went into the cool interior and sat on the mats in the shade, near the potted plants.

After a respectful pause, Mahmoud began. "*I have come to ask you more questions about this man, Jesus. He has piqued my curiosity*", he said.

"*Ask anything you will, my friend, I can only try to reply*", said Sergius, linking his fingers in the lap of his robe.

"*You had said that his mother was Miriam, that he was born without a human father. How could this be?*"

"*Can we limit the power of the One who moves the stars and the earth, who sends the rain and causes the crops to grow? Is such a small thing as a virginal birth impossible to Him?*"

"*No, indeed*", mused Mahmoud. "*Miriam must have found favour in His sight. She must have been a most perfect woman*".

"*Indeed so*", said the monk, "*that is why we honour her as "Mother of Christ", the Anointed One, the Messiah*"

"*But I have heard that the Christians of Roma go further than that. That they call her "Mother of God", that Jesus is "He-Who-Is".*"

"*True, true*", said Sergius, shaking his head, "*and that is why our teaching was condemned by the Roumi over one hundred and seventy years ago. There may be a long road to go yet before we understand one another perfectly. But of this we are certain, that Jesus is the Messiah foretold by the prophets of the Hebrews, that he died crucified, according to Roman Law…….."*

"Excuse me, but how could your All-Powerful God permit such a thing? Could He not have lifted just one little finger to save his Messiah, He whom you say is capable of regulating the movements of the heavens?"

"Certainly, but who are we to dictate to Him a course of action? Even the ancient Prophets of the Hebrews spoke of such a shameful death for the Servant of the Lord (a). Is He not free to allow such a terrible thing so that all humanity may be saved?"

"How, "saved"?"

"Yes, saved from moral weakness, from sin, and above all from eternal death and separation from "He-Who-Is". For three days later Jesus rose from the dead……"

Mahmoud rose in a rush. *"Pardon me"* he said heatedly, *"but this I cannot accept. That one should be sent, should suffer for many, yes. But for such a one to die, certainly not. God must have put some sinner in his place on the cross, perhaps Judas, the traitor you once spoke about, so I cannot accept that your Messiah died. And as for rising again, no man can return from the grave. You die when you die, and that's the end of the story."*

"But the scriptures, the witnesses, all attest to this. They saw and spoke with him, ate with him, touched him……"

"Lies, all lies! Falsifications all! Did you not once tell me that it was women who first brought the news?"

"Yes," said the monk.

"There you are! The rantings of sensitive grief-stricken weaklings! What God would present himself first to women? The very idea is absurd!" He sat again, and waited, breathing hard.

The monk began patiently again, after a pause.

"Compared to what the most ancient Scriptures say, would you not admit that your protestations seem purely gratuitous?"

"Perhaps so, but compared to the absurdities I have heard, they seem more reasonable. Jesus was a great prophet, but he did not die on the cross. Nor did he rise again, as you claim. He was not divine".

"The ways of God are mysterious, my son. Is it not a question of Faith in the impossible"?

"Not only the impossible, Abuna Sergius, but the totally incomprehensible." He paused. *"You once spoke to me of the Trinity, of three Persons in God Himself, didn't you? Now, how can you expect me to believe in that which is in itself unbelievable? Frankly, I am surprised that you yourself should continue to be a monk and believe in such impossibilities, when Yahweh – the One God – of the Hebrews makes more sense, is so much more reasonable."*

"Perhaps you are in danger of reducing the One God to the level of mere human reasoning, Mahmoud, when in fact He is totally beyond it. His Being cannot be comprehended by our limited ways of thought, nor is His existence to be compared to ours." He paused again. "But tell me, you have heard of Yahweh?", he asked in surprise.

"Yes, I have also discussed about Him with Eleazar, the Chief Rabbi who heads the synagogue in Makka (b). *I understand that you have your differences with him also?"*

"Alas, yes. Our teachings differ radically. If only they too may receive the gift of Faith, and would accept Jesus as the foretold Messiah! They wait for his first coming, we await his second".

"And I, Abuna Sergius?"

"Yes, and you, Mahmoud. You are not far from the truth. It is up to you to ask for the gifts of faith in prayer. I too shall pray for you and your search for it. Who knows? Perhaps one day you will find it". He sighed, then rose and blessed the pensive Arab. *"Now go, with my blessing and friendship".*

They embraced. Mahmoud called for his camel, mounted, gave a sign of farewell, and was gone. *Abuna* Sergius sighed again as he left. He was so impetuous, this man of the desert....

They were not to meet again.

He had been an illiterate camel-driver for a rich widow whom he eventually married, but he was a seeker for meaning in life. He vaguely suspected that all the idols and gods – Habul, Al-uzza, Manat, Al-lat, among others – of the many Arab tribes of which he formed part, were false, and so he had spent much time in the bazaars among the Hebrew and Nestorian merchants, learning of their Faiths.

Though illiterate, Mahmoud had the gift of memory, as had so many others of the people of the desert, the result of many centuries of retaining the oral traditions of his people. He thus recalled most of the facts he had learned from the Hebrews, especially the belief that the Messiah was yet to come. He had even made friends with one or other of the learned Rabbis, and became familiar with the stories of Moses, of the angels, of the history of these People. He had learned of Yahweh, of the Prophets, of the Messiah who was to come, of David, Solomon, of the Evil One, of eternal life, of eternal punishment, of the Hebrew Law. He had been particularly impressed with the story of Abraham and the near-sacrifice of his son Isaac on the Hill of Moriah.

But he had been dissatisfied with the Rabbis and their Law. It seemed so unfinished. It seemed as though they were forever waiting....and so he had begun searching elsewhere.

He had then befriended the Nestorian Christian monk Sergius, and to his amazement found that the story had come full circle with the birth of Jesus. He learnt of the Virgin Birth, of Miriam, of Joseph, of the miracles and tremendous claims of this Hebrew Teacher.

But he was troubled and had many doubts. He could accept Jesus as a great Prophet, perhaps the greatest of all, but how could he swallow the claims that he was the Son of God – for "Allah" had no wife!, – that he had died and returned to life, that in God there were Three Persons....how could he, illiterate and uninstructed, understand and believe all that the Christians claimed to be true ? What should he believe then?

Uni had not been there when Mahmoud had wed, when he had befriended the Nestorians and the Hebrews, or the monk Sergius, when he had undergone his terrible soul-searching to find true meaning to life.... He had pieced together all this from the camels and horses of his caravans, visiting their enclosures at night, or even in daylight, in the form of a faint blue haze....and he had taken to following Mahmoud in his visits to the Rabbis and to the *Abuna* Sergius.....

So it was with great care that he followed Mahmoud into the desert one day where he entered a cave to pray in the manner of the Nestorian monks, touching his forehead to the ground in adoration before the God-Who-Sees-All, the God-Who-Knows-All, the All-powerful, the Eternal....

And it was there that Uni saw the transformation....

During his meditation, all of a sudden Mahmoud jerked from his low stool and fell forward on his mat. His limbs stiffened and his head rolled backwards on his stiffened neck muscles. His eyes remained open and strange phrases began coming from his lips... *"There..is...no..God..but..Allah.....no God...but...Allah.....you...me? me? I? I? ......I. am .his.. prophet?.... There is no God but Allah, and I, Mahmoud, am his prophet?.... The prophet???.....of Allah the clement, the merciful???? ...Ahhhhhh......* Then he slumped forward and curled into a ball, exhausted.

The Unicorn had seen people in trance before in his many travels. It would not last long, and so he waited patiently as Mahmoud slowly came to. He looked dazedly around as full consciousness returned, then washed his face from the skin gourd he carried. He drank deeply, and shortly afterwards untethered his camel and rode away. He kept repeating the phrase to himself *"There is no God but Allah, and I am his prophet".* The Unicorn realised that something extraordinary had happened. Mahmoud seemed to have received a message and was convinced that he had become the Messenger of God – his Prophet.

In subsequent visits to the cave, the Unicorn came close enough to Mahmoud to hear him utter the names of those he had learned about in the Books of the Hebrews and of the Christians....Gabriel the Angel...David....Jesus...Miriam...Anna...Joseph... Solomon....the names became more and more frequent as Mahmoud continued his visits. He seemed to be clarifying his thoughts, and prayed often as before, touching his forehead to the ground in adoration as he usually did, Nestorian fashion.

He returned once with several friends, and told them that he had received a message from Allah the Clement, the Merciful, through Gabriel his Angel. The message was that he was the last of the Prophets, that all must be brought to believe in One God, that all must admit that

"There is no God but God, and Mahmoud is his prophet".

The Unicorn followed all this with great interest. There were now going to be three spiritual forces in the vastness of Arabia! The Hebrews had for centuries settled in Makka, Yathrib (c) and other places, often rubbing shoulders with the Nestorian

Christians, and now a new Faith was to enter on the scene. How would they get on together? Could they co-exist?

He saw the men listening intently and taking note of Mahmoud's words whenever they met. He saw their amazement as the implications of the words of the illiterate camel-driver-become-Prophet sank in, saw them planning to carry the Message outwards.

Events moved swiftly after that. Mahmoud had to flee for his life from Makka when Arab adorers of the local gods threw him out, and spent some time further north in Yathrib, where he was able to convince the folk of his calling. He then returned with an armed group to Makka, took it, threw out the idols in the Kaaba building, and made it his centre of operations. He slaughtered the Hebrews in Makka, who had refused to accept him as the Prophet of Allah.

The Unicorn saw Mahmoud organise and unify the warring tribes into an efficient fighting force, and soon the conquest for Allah had begun.

Over the next hundred years after Mahmoud's death (d), he saw the armies of Allah occupy Palestine and take control of the Holy Places (e) where the Child of Bethlehem had walked. He saw them sweep to the north into Europa, into Greece, Turkey, Asia Minor. Having taken Alexandria in Egypt to the south (f), they reached Ethiopia without being able to conquer it (g), and then swept westwards along the north African coast. They encountered there the many Christian Communities already established for over six hundred years. Heavy tribute was paid by the peaceful and unprepared Christians to be allowed to practise their Faith (h). Non-payment alternated with forced conversion or execution, and in a relatively short two hundred years later Christianity had all but disappeared from these lands through the constant fanatical pressure of the well-organised invaders.

The religion of the Arabs – "Islam" or "submission to Allah"- was taking hold fast, and seemed invincible and unstoppable.

The Warriors of Allah then streamed across the Straits of Djabel-al-Tariq (i) into the Spanish peninsula (j) and installed themselves firmly there before moving northwards. At first, they were victorious, but were defeated by Christian armies near the French city of Poitiers (k). They then retreated into Spain and remained there for almost eight centuries (l), being finally driven out by the united Christian forces of the Spanish Sovereigns Ferdinand and Isabella, into north Africa (m).

Uni the Unicorn saw them resettle along the north-African coast and in the interior regions. In North and West Africa centres of Islamic learning developed here and there in the vast expanses of the areas bordering the Great Desert (n), and also in the land of the Pyramid-Builders (o).

But their intellectual efforts were mainly limited to the study of the holy book of Islam, the Qur'an (p) and Islamic Canon Law (q). No purely civil schools were set up for the ordinary folk, learning was confined to the Koranic texts in the *madrasas* (r), and so the vast majority of Africans remained as ignorant and superstitious as they had been before Islam arrived. This situation was to last for many centuries....

During all this time the Unicorn was able to follow the fortunes of the Christian Ecclesia – the One, Holy, Catholic, Apostolic Church with Roma as its centre, as the Christians maintained – and its influence in Europa. The word "Catholic"- Universal – had been used from early years in Syria.

Ecclesia had in fact succeeded in salvaging the best of what had remained of the Roman Empire. Roman Law, Roman culture, Roman administration, architecture, language, all were taken up and given new meaning.

Churches and vast basilicas were built, taking as their models the ancient pagan temples of Jupiter, Apollo, Diana. Greek, then Latin – the version spoken in the streets of Roma by ordinary folk – became the common language of Ecclesia, and even the ceremonial dress of the Senators and other government officials had been adapted for its official cult and prayer. With growing amazement, the Unicorn realized that the end of the Roman Empire had not meant the end of civilisation, but rather the start of a new one, where people and their values had become more important than before, with the words of the Child and the Good News as guide.

With the end of the orgies and bacchanalia, the forbidding of the practice of infanticide, divorce and polygamy, Uni could see that little by little the level of morality was improving among the population. Intermittent wars and feuds among the powerful Roman families gradually dwindled to a trickle, and because of all these changes Ecclesia began to be universally admired among the people.

He wondered – how long would this last? How far could it go?

Chapter 17
Travels To The Sun

But wander-lust was in Uni's blood, so he left the struggling west and headed to the lands from where the sun rose. He crossed the dry deserts and the tree-covered mountains, swam the icy waters of the tumbling rivers, played with the wild onagers in the hills, passed through the bamboo forests where the placid pandas munched away on the young shoots, ran again with the upland yaks, and finally arrived at the land of Confucius the Sage, the Philosopher, the Law-Giver.....

Swishhhhh! Thud! The arrow slammed into the tree near him, and he saw the archer taking aim again. Like a bolt he was gone from there, where men could hurt from afar, and doubled his watch-fulness as he visited this country of new experiences.

He marvelled at the strange buildings with their curved roofs, the flowing vestments with tassels, the temples, the ornamental pools with shining gold and silver fish. He heard the new sing-song language and found that it came to him as naturally as the others he had learned in the west. There were horses there too, beautiful animals with proud heads and impatient stamping feet. He drew near to them and learned that this vast country was called Cathay, land of the yellow men (a).

This was a land much given to conflict among the warlords of each region, and to his horror he witnessed the incredibly sadistic tortures to which prisoners were submitted – the bamboo torture, where fast-growing bamboo from below literally skewered the spread-eagled body of the unfortunate captive in just one day; the fishing-net torture, where fleshy parts of the prisoner protruding from the fishing-net which tightly bound him were systematically sliced off; the water-drop torture, where the man gradually went insane as drops of water fell onto his forehead at irregular intervals; and there was the flaying, the impaling, and others which made his blood run cold. But the crowds came for amusement...just as the Romans had done for entertainment on the elevated seats of the Colosseum...

And yet these were intelligent and sophisticated people. They had invented the amazing magnetic needle which always pointed to the cold regions of the Aurora Borealis, and a powder which they used to make brilliant displays of lights and loud bangs in the sky at night. And their counting frames with little balls clicking to and fro under their agile fingers – these and other marvels were quite unknown to the Unicorn, as were the fat worms from whose silken threads the people of Cathay wove their soft shimmering robes.

Will the West ever get to know of these wonders? he mused.

Separated from the temples of Confucius, here and there wooden temple bells bonked and boomed. Shaven *bonzes* (b) in saffron robes hummed and chanted their endless praise of the Enlightened One, the Buddha (c). *"Oooommm! Oooommm! Ooommm mane padme hooommm! Oh, the Jewel in the Lotus!"* Over and over again they chanted their *mantras* and spun their prayer-wheels, while in the dusty streets other monks collected their daily food offerings from the kneeling faithful, as their religion decreed.

A peaceful people, these Buddhists, but has the concept of "He-Who-Is" ever crossed their minds?, thought the Unicorn, as he left their country, heading towards the south, to the land of the brown people of the coast.

He had been there many centuries before, and found that time seemed to have stood still. Practically nothing had changed, in contrast to what was going on in Europa.......

But compared to the soberness of the northern peoples, Uni was buoyed up by the vibrancy of the southerners, the Hindus. Statues of their many gods were still everywhere. He heard the names of Vishnu, Shiva, Kali, Rama, Nandi, and the greatest of all, Durga, and so many others, all the time. There were always processions meandering through the streets with clanging cymbals and booming drums, the dancers leaping and beating their chests or flagellating themselves before the statue of their god on its dais. The brightly coloured robes of the women outshone the simple *capra* (d) of the men, and the nasal high-pitched singing took some getting used to. It was clear that this Hindu religion was something to be taken seriously and enjoyed at the same time. In the narrow dusty streets skinny cows roamed and ambled at will. They were sacred to the Hindus, Uni found, and were not to be eaten nor allowed to suffer in any way. They were in fact incarnations of one of their divinities.

Uni blue-hazed himself, and began to wander among the fortune-tellers and magicians of these people. Searching for one's destiny seemed to be the great preoccupation of the Hindus, both in the cities and villages. Magicians, snake-charmers, astrologers, emaciated fakirs denying all pain on their beds of nails or with skewers punched through their bloodless cheeks, all jostled in the multi-coloured crowds in the narrow streets, either coming from or going to prayers before one god or the other.

On a nearby riverbank a funeral pyre was just being set alight, the chanting priests throwing gobs of yellow butter on the logs to help them catch fire. The thin cotton covering the corpse on top burned away soon, revealing a man's body. It began to writhe and sizzle as the fire took hold.

A scream, and a young woman in yellow dashed from the crowd and climbed some unburnt logs to the top, then threw herself across the dead body. Her long hair flamed up and disappeared, then her robes, and finally her body too twisted in agony and screaming under the fierce flames and smoke. *"Suttee! Suttee!"*, screamed the women around the pyre. *"Go with your husband, so does Shiva wish it!"*. The blue haze turned away as the two bodies were consumed, united in life, united in death.

And yet, pondered the Unicorn as he left this amazing country behind and trotted further east, this people of many gods are expert mathematicians and geographers.

I have seen their priests and teachers at work, he mused, *and swear that I have not seen the like in the countries of the west. But it seems that, as I noticed so long ago, that the ordinary people still have to be satisfied with their manifold gods, their sacrifices, and their processions. How strange indeed, compared to the belief in the Messiah of the Hebrews and the Christians, in the one God who calls Himself "I-Am-Who-Am"*.

Then he came to the furthest land to the east, Xi-Pangu (e), swimming across the stretch of water as before. He had returned to the place he had once visited many centuries ago, and he found that the country was now under the control of many *shogun* warlords, each with his own private army. Here there were no multicoloured crowds as before, nor shaven *bonzes* chanting their *"Ooommm, Ooommm"* in the land of yellow people. As yet no one single chief had unified the country. Anarchy reigned.

But the many shrines to the dead, with burning perfume-sticks stuck in sand, convinced the Unicorn that here too, death and destiny were major preoccupations of these people. They hoped for peace and rest after a life given to drudgery and worry, and the simple shrines to their departed, the prayers on coloured rice-paper burnt in the shrines, touched the Unicorn's heart as never before.

He wished their future well as he continued even further east, crossing again large stretches of water and ice-floes, avoiding the huge white polar-bears and the even larger brown grizzlies fishing for salmon in the rivers. He eventually came upon the endless plains of a new land where herds of wild bison roamed. These were the lands of the copper people.

CHAPTER 18
West Goes East

They were indeed generally copper-skinned, burnt by the summer sun and cooled by the winter cold, their skins taking on a rich coppery colour. They oiled themselves regularly with buffalo fat until their skins gleamed in the sun and in the campfire's glow. Their tribes lived in the hills or on the plains, hunting the buffalo and deer for their food, their clothing and their religion. The Unicorn heard many languages among them, and saw that in general each tribe kept to its own territory and its customs. There was space enough for everyone, and so conflicts rarely arose among them. When they did, these normally lasted for only short periods, and palavers were held and the Pipe of Peace was smoked....

As he wandered among the tribes of the copper-people, Uni thought-spoke with the many ponies they had captured from the wild herds of horses on the plains, hardy little animals whose ultimate cooking-pot destiny they shared with the scrawny dogs of the tribe. These ponies had wandered much and learned much.

From them the Unicorn learned that to the permanently ice-bound north were the Inuit. These people dressed in warm furs throughout the year, lived in round ice-houses, hunted the great whale, the seal and the bear, and fished for salmon under the ice. They skimmed over the freezing water among the floes in their rapid seal-skin *kayaks*, and abandoned their aged on the shelves of ice to be killed and eaten by the great white bear, their chief divinity. Thus, they would rejoin their ancestors.

On the immense spaces lived the people of the plains, the Sioux, the Algonquins, the Cheyenne, and the many sub-tribes. On the rivers and coasts lived the Mohawks, in the mountains to the south were the fierce Apache feared by all for their raids on the plains people for food and mates, and to the very far south in the wetlands were the Seminole. The Unicorn marvelled at all this information, but the piebald pony he talked with had travelled widely, and shared his knowledge willingly.

Even further to the warmer south, his friend the pony had heard of tribes (a) who lived in stone houses. They made war continually on their neighbours, and sacrificed their prisoners, male, female and even the very young, on great stone pyramids, cutting out the pumping heart from the breasts of their victims with stone knives. For their insatiable gods (b) demanded human blood for the crops, for fertility, for life, for the sun's daily rising. These peoples had no horses to ride or to work the land, nor buffalo to hunt or to eat, but grew a vast variety of plants and crops, some of which had become gods, so essential were they for their survival (c).

And even further downwards to the south, the pony seemed to be uncertain*, *live many tribes in the deep wet forests. Their lives are secret, so no one knows much about them. Though they are said to be expert hunters and archers, yet no one knows them or their gods*, he admitted.

As for what the copper people call god, he thought-spoke, *here there are many names for the Great Spirit, but most call him "Manitou", "He-Who Sustains", and they sacrifice dogs to it, some-times even a horse, but never one of their own*.

How strange, thought the Unicorn to himself, *wherever I go I have found different tribes and peoples, customs and languages. I have seen these copper people, the yellow men, the brown men, the black ones, and the white and cream coloured. And yet they are no different one from the other, and in every tribe, there seems to be a Big Question about a Great Spirit, a Sustainer, One who gives meaning to life. I have never found a single nation without such a question, which didn't make sacrifices to a mystery. This is a great problem for me. Where could such an idea have come from?*

Tell me, he continued to the pony, *where do all these copper people come from? They resemble the yellow people, but they clearly are not the same. How did they come to be here?*

According to what the ancients say around the campfires at night, explained the pony, *their ancestors indeed came down from the lands around the countries of the yellow people. They walked eastwards across the ice and land (d) by tribes and families to find new pastures, new lands for their peoples. This went on for many, many years, and as they came to the east some settled in the frozen lands, some came to the great plains where we are now, and others kept going to the sun slanting on the horizon, where it is much warmer than here, where it is never cold.* He paused, then continued.

As time went by the tribes and families grew and separated and filled the spaces you now see. They are happy here; they hunt and fish and can grow. But their life is short and their sicknesses many, and the most they can hope for is to repose in the Happy Hunting Ground, in which they all believe.

The Unicorn thought about this and decided to change the subject. *And what lies in the direction of the rising sun from where we are? Are there more lands and peoples over there? What is to be found there?*

There is no more land there, One-Horn, only water. Water as far as the eye can see, and even beyond. Even the smell of land – if there were land over there – has never reached us here, so I am sure that it is the edge of the world. Only salty water and more salty water (e). You've reached the end of your journey, it seems.

Yes, so it does, my friend, admitted the Unicorn. *And so, I will leave you and yours. You cannot come with me, for I have very far to go and you could never keep up with me.

I shall return to the most interesting place of all, to Europa, where the Big Question – the meaning of life – of all the peoples and tribes I have visited, seems to have found an answer*.

I shall return to Roma, where a group calling themselves "Christians" are proclaiming their belief that the Great Spirit himself became a human person, a man. They say that this man was killed by his enemies, but three days later he came back to life, and now offers eternal life to all who believe in and accept him, for he can no longer die. I myself saw this man when he had been newly-born, he paused, remembering the touch of the Child so many centuries ago in the grotto of Bethlehem….

He continued. **The movement has aroused great interest in the lands where the people of Europa live, and I have no doubt but that it will reach other lands and other peoples and tribes, because they all seem to have the same Big Question – why am I here ? where am I going ? what is the purpose of life? what lies beyond death? Perhaps one day it may even come here, to the lands of the copper people. Who can tell the future? Not even I……**

The Unicorn paused. **And when I leave, what will happen to you, my friend? Will you escape and rejoin your brothers on the plains?**

When I am not in this corral, I am hobbled, so I cannot go far, One-Horn, thought-spoke the pony, **so I can never escape. I did so once, but I was caught again and brought back, so I have no urge to do so again. The copper people are far too clever!**

So…..?

So, I shall continue to serve until I die. Perhaps I shall end as a meal in my owner's wigwam, perhaps I shall be let loose on the plains as a reward, as they sometimes do. But whatever it may be, I shall certainly die! He had no sadness in his thought-speech. **It is the law of life*.*

He paused. **Now go on your way, One-Horn. I bid you farewell*.* He whinnied softly, turned and went to the far end of the enclosure and looked away in the opposite direction.

The Unicorn's stay had come to an end. It had been over two hundred years since leaving the west, and now it was time to go back, to see how Ecclesia in Europa had developed in the meantime, and how it was coping with the Warriors of Allah and their new teaching. He whinnied in a farewell reply, and when the piebald pony looked again to where he had been, the dust was already settling.

CHAPTER 19

East Goes West

The further he left the Great Plains behind, the more the Unicorn recognized the land he'd crossed so many years before. Untroubled by the cold and unworried by fatigue, he tirelessly trotted on through what was one day to become Canada, clitter-clattering along the mountain paths, swimming in the rivers fed by the melting snows. The grizzlies showed their fangs at him as he paused to admire their fishing technique, and the deer moose with their two-yard-wide antlers stared at One-Horn in his shiny white coat as he ran past. They "whuffed" in challenge, but he was already gone.

And so he crossed the land bridges joining east to west, and arrived into the tundra of farthest Asia. Down he went into Mongolia where the descendants of the original herds of yaks and Bactrian camels (a) stared as he paused in salute. But they had never been out of their country, and apart from polite greetings, conversation was limited. He left.

Then through Cathay again, where he found that the Nestorian Christians had arrived far into the interior, to a place called Xi-An, – and he realized that this was already the eighth century "after Bethlehem"! So, Ecclesia was on the move, it seemed. He hurried on to the countries of the south.

There in the Land of Wisdom, of the brown people, he met Christians who had been taught by a certain "Mar Thoma", whom he decided must have been the same tired Traveller he'd met on the road so many centuries before (b), and he marvelled at the speed of expansion of the Message of the Messiah. It seemed to him that his prediction would one day be realized. It would perhaps go everywhere, perhaps one day even to the lands of the copper people....

He reached Roma. Roma, the centre of the Christian Faith in the west, that had so nearly been destroyed by the armed horsemen from Siberia (c), but for the intervention of the then Fisherman (d). But it was now over a thousand years "after Bethlehem", and Uni observed that Ecclesia was continuing to proclaim the Good News of the Messiah, his death and Resurrection, as before. She still continued to convoke Councils, in Roma itself, as well as in other important places, and to clarify and reaffirm the deposit of Faith against those who would water it down or interpret it otherwise, and kept on sending her missionaries to foreign lands as before.

The centuries passed, and there came and went many "Peters" to the Chair of the First Fisherman. Many had given their lives for the Faith, some had died in exile, others had languished in prison until death had claimed them. Most had been worthy holders of the Fisherman's post, while some had been less so....

Meanwhile, for administrative purposes, years were now being counted as coming after the birth of the Child of Bethlehem. So instead of calculating time from such and such an Emperor's birth or death, it was now "Anno Domini", in the "Year of the Lord". It became clear to Uni that Ecclesia was also exercising a strong political influence in the day-to-day running of the State.

But even Ecclesia was not exempt from the lure of worldly power, and eventually she was to fall prey to the underhand dealings of nepotism, the pull of riches, and the rivalries among the ancient and powerful families around Roma, each of which wanted its own "Peter" on the throne of the Fisherman. There came many cries for reform, but Ecclesia read the signs of the times badly, and reform, though agreed to in principle, and encouraged by great thinkers and saints, was not a major preoccupation of the Fishermen for many years.

The problem which most troubled Ecclesia in the fourteenth and fifteenth centuries "A. D." was the growing power of Islam. This new religion had made serious inroads into the Christian countries in the east, and had taken over the Lebanon, Palestine, Syria, Turkey, the countries of the Baltic, Albania, parts of the Slavonic States, and of course, Egypt and northern Africa. Islam then went on to occupy the Far East, settling in Afghanistan, India, China, and Mongolia, as well as in many countries of the Russian interior. Decidedly, it had become a force to be reckoned with.

In these former Christian countries now controlled by Islam, many were the conversions to the new faith, many were the martyrs. The Unicorn learned that the *"jizya"* tax was imposed upon Christians so that they could be "protected" and thus practise their Faith undisturbed among the Faithful of Allah, but constant relentless pressure was brought upon them to convert. By bribe, forced marriages and subtle menace or even open threats, Christianity gave way to Islam in these countries. Many Christians gave in for the sake of peace, so as not to be considered as outcasts, as second-class citizens, and to find employment.

To the Unicorn it seemed that Islam, which claimed to be the religion of mutual love, pardon, and respect for the conscience of the individual, had given way to the sword, the violation of personal rights, the relegation of women to second-class citizenship. But the major change came with the negation of the main tenets of the Christian Faith, such as he was able to understand them – the Holy Trinity and the relationship between Father, Son, and Holy Spirit, was denied, the Child of Bethlehem was not the Second Person of the Trinity become Man – and so he was not "He-Who-Is" – the Sacraments were out, Mary was not the "Theotokos"(e), and so on....

But the toleration of Christianity by Islam continued, to the benefit of the latter, more so in the former land of the Chosen People, than elsewhere. Having taken over by force most of the shrines and places which had been frequented by the Messiah and mentioned in the Book of Books, the Christian Bible, the *muslin* (f) rulers of the Holy Land levied heavy taxes on Christian pilgrims wishing to visit these places, and there were cases of beatings and abduction, even though safe-conduct passes had been guaranteed. These were the beginnings of the reasons for the Crusades......

These Crusades, eight in all, were born out of a sense of frustration and hurt by the Christian peoples of Europa, who saw Islam as usurper and enemy. Though many would die on both sides in the forthcoming battles, yet a call to take up arms was preached both by "Peter" in Roma and by great Saints, to which Christian nobility and ordinary folk eagerly responded.

The Unicorn saw the first Crusaders leave as a disorganised crowd, all of whom were massacred by the Turks (g). The following Crusade was more organized and soldierly, and led to the establishment of the Latin Kingdom of Jerusalem (h), after the massacre of the entire Muslim population of the Holy City. But this Kingdom lasted only a relatively short time, during which the Crusaders built castles strongly and widely, European style, throughout the Holy Land. But they were finally driven out by the sheer numbers and flexibility of the Islamic troops (i).

But even before the Crusades had begun, there had been acrimonious discussions among the theologians of Roma and those of Constantinople, with its thousand-year prestige as seat of the eastern half of Ecclesia, concerning the nature of the Holy Trinity. This ended in both sides excommunicating one another (j), which sad state of affairs continued when the Crusades eventually began.

Frustrated with the failure to take the Holy Places with relative ease, and also because no help was forthcoming from Constantinople, in the thirteenth century A.D. the great City was overrun by another group of Crusaders, with widespread massacres of both Christians and *muslins* in the city itself. It became a Latin Kingdom (k) ruled according to the Roman Rite, to the great rage of the Easterners, who had long had their own language and liturgy (l). This Kingdom was not to last, and eventually Constantinople was restored to them.

Apart from the animosity caused between Christianity and Islam, the final break in relationships between the authority of the Fisherman in Roma and the Patriarch in Constantinople was the worst result of the Crusades. There had been no apologies from either the Crusaders, or from Roma for that matter, for the massacres committed there, and the mutual excommunications did nothing to help. The Unicorn wondered if this were not the beginning of the end for Ecclesia as a meaningful body.

The final Crusades were mainly disorganised and quarrelsome, and were completely wiped out by the Warriors of Allah. The most pathetic of all was the "Children's Crusade", when thousands of children led by several young "prophets", set out to retake the Holy Places in the Holy Land. All were captured and sold into slavery in Egypt (m), and Jerusalem was lost for ever to the Christian cause

All of this information had come to the Unicorn by hearsay, so he decided to go to the Holy Land to see the situation for himself. To the Land where he had first seen the Child....

He trotted by night and took it easy by day in the mountains where few people went, except for the woodcutter who caught a glimpse of him once in Greece and alerted the villagers. But a certain blue haze caused them to ridicule the man for having cried *"Wolf!"*. *"Retsina wine does that sometimes!"* they laughed, as they shouldered their weapons and went home. The blue haze suppressed a chuckle....

The situation in the Holy Land was even worse than he had expected. The main places where the Child had taught and prayed were now solidly in Muslim hands, as the followers of Mahmoud were now called. The ancient Temple emplacement now sported a glittering mosque, built by Christian architects, using the columns left over from destroyed Christian churches (n). The Bezatha and Siloë pools, the Cenacle, the Basilica of the Holy Sepulchre, the Church of the Ascension, all these were now controlled by Islam. Even the grotto of the Nativity of the Virgin, over which the Crusaders had built an imposing Basilica, could not be visited except by bribes and the indignity of being let down into the grotto beneath, through a hole pierced under the foundations.

Uni left with a heavy heart. He could do nothing but observe, and started on the return journey, to Europa, where Ecclesia and the new Christian States were often to come into conflict.

CHAPTER 20

Memory

It was in the mountains of Greece that he saw the white Owl looking at him fixedly. And then the thought-message came - *What a strange creature is this!*

Uni of course could read the owl's surprise, so he thought-spoke in reply – *Why do you call me strange, old Owl?*

The Owl nearly tumbled off his branch as the Unicorn's thought-words reached him, then he blinked his two huge yellow eyes as only owls can, and exclaimed – *Well, what a surprise! A talking horse!*

I'm not a horse, Owl, I'm the One-Horn.

So you are! In fact, I was wondering about that horn. How did it get there? And what's it for?

Since I can remember, no one has ever told me what my horn was for. I had to find that out for myself.

And what did you find, One-Horn?

I've found that it can make me near-invisible, like this. He touched a rock with his horn, and at once became a faint blue mist. *Do you understand?* came the thought-voice from the mist.

Amazing! I can just barely see where you are. And to come back...?

He touched the rock again, and stood there looking up at the Owl. *As simple as that*.

Marvellous! I've never seen the like! And what else can your horn do?

It can strengthen people and heal wounds. I've often used it at night among the dying and wounded on the battlefields. The poor soldiers must have thought I was an apparition, but I had left before they had fully come to. And I once helped a Traveller of "He-Who-Is" to find the courage to continue his voyage into the mountains....

Incredible! But where do you yourself come from? Are there more like you? Forgive me for asking, but....

Not at all, thought-spoke Uni the Unicorn. *When I was born many, many centuries ago I vaguely remember a blue light from the sky shining on me. It came every night for a whole month,* and *in that month I remember growing to be as big as my own mother. She was not a One-Horn, so it must have been the light that gave it to me*.

But where did all this take place, One-Horn?

It was a very warm place, near the Great Lakes of Africa, and there were many huge lizards around, some as big as houses. And there were enormous volcanoes and storms most of the time, and a lot of rain. This went on for a long time, until the meteor fell from the sky and changed the whole Earth completely (a).

Tell me some more about the Blue Light.

As I said, it came every nightfall from the sky to where I was with my mother, and I could not move as it played over my back and shoulders and eventually my whole body. But it remained on the spot on my forehead where the Horn grew and grew every night, to be what it is today.

And what else did the Blue Light do?

Well, it has given me strength and extraordinary resistance to fatigue. I can go for many days without tiring, and I only need a minimum of food and rest. Also, I do not seem to have grown any older, even though I have lived many lifetimes and seen most of the world.

And….? pursued the Owl.

And I can easily thought-speak with both animal and man, and have been doing so since man evolved on the Earth. And that is why I can communicate with you!

Extraordinary! But, where did the Blue Light go? Or did it ever come again?

No, it went away as strangely as it had come. Through all these years I have often wondered about this Light, but I have no idea where it came from or where it has gone. I only know that I am what I am because of it.

It seems then that you are indeed the only One-Horn, or have you met others of your kind on your travels?

No, I seem to be the only one in the world, but that is not to say that I have not searched.

The Owl paused for thought. Then began again. *Can you say what is the meaning of your life, One-Horn? After all, you seem indestructible, you have lived far longer than any other living being, you have received extraordinary gifts, and yet, what do you make of it all? What is the reason for your being that way? What are you here for?*

Uni the Unicorn paced to and fro in the clearing as he tried to reason that out. The Owl had posed a fundamental question, one that he had asked himself many times – what in fact was the *real* meaning of his life, of his incessant travelling, of his gifts? The Owl waited patiently as the Unicorn gathered his thoughts.

He took a long time to reply, closing his eyes as if passing in review all the centuries of changes, experiences, dangers, and peoples he'd met or the climates he'd passed through. Rapidly his thoughts crystallized into a single searing point, and try as he would, he was unable to get it out of his mind. At last he opened his eyes and began to speak.

In the first place, friend Owl, through no merit or choice on my part, I seem to be the only One-Horn that will probably ever exist. In all the centuries of my life, I have gathered more information about the world and its peoples, its languages, the plants and animals, its climates, than any other living being. But you ask – Why all this?

Well, I don't seem to have been of much use to the world as such, except on very rare occasions. My incredible gifts have been in general my protection. My horn can give me near-invisibility, my thought-speech has allowed me to speak to either men or animals. I need little food or rest, and my speed gives me the power to cover great distances without pausing, and I am practically immune to climate change. I can be wounded, perhaps even killed, but so far neither has happened…although I have been captured once, in China, and only escaped by hazing myself in time. So, I see myself not as having been put on the Earth to be useful, nor even to resolve problems.

No, I prefer to see myself as a collector of data from all over. What eventually all this is to be used for is unknown to me, but I am able to recall down to the smallest detail all that I have seen, met or experienced through all these centuries. If I close my eyes, I can see again my mother's sadness as I left her, the fall of the meteor and the end of the lizard-kings, the slow evolution from animal to man, the old man who almost sacrificed his only son, the Child in his little crib in Bethlehem. The peoples of China, India, Japan, the copper men of America. And I experience again the rise and fall of Greece and Roma, the start of Ecclesia, Nestor, Mahmoud, the Islamic conquests. My life has been extremely rich and varied, indeed.

In a word, I am Memory, so that what has gone before should not be forgotten. Perhaps one day I shall understand, but for the present I am still in the dark as to the real use of this gift of Memory. As far as I can see, the world is changing day by day, century by century, so I suppose I still have a lot of experiences to live through and to memorize.

Fair enough, One-Horn. And now, just one more question. Where are you going from here?

I'm on my way to Europa, to see what is going to happen between the Christian peoples and those of Islam. I have just returned from the land of the Child of Bethlehem, and I have seen how there have been forced conversions, constant humiliation of the Christians, the tax on the dhimmi, exile for the unwilling, and even forced marriages. To me all this seems strange, coming from a religion which believes in a "clement and merciful" God (b). And in Syria there is the Old Man of the Mountain, who trains assassins through doping them with hashish. A strange lot indeed, it seems to me….

So, it's off to Europa you are, and then…?

I cannot really tell, but I think that I will stay there permanently. The peoples of the Far East do not seem to have anything new to say to the world, with their many deities and their ancestor cults and their philosophies. They seem to be turning in circles, as are the peoples of Africa, unfortunately.

The most interesting thing at present, it seems to me, is the belief in a Man who died and rose again. This is in itself is an enormous message of hope for humanity all over. The only trouble is, that there is tremendous opposition to this in Islam, which not only denies that the Child died on the Cross, but that he even rose again from the dead. So, as I see it, these two points of view are irreconcilable, which means interesting centuries ahead.

So it seems, One-Horn, so it seems. And now I will leave you to continue your travels. He spread his wings…...

One question, old Owl. How come you were able to ask such deep questions? This has been the first time……

Didn't you know? In Greece they call me the Bird of Wisdom, and that's why you'll find me stamped on their coins! Fare you well, One-Horn, I enjoyed our talk. And his soft feathers took him silently away into the dark mountains.

Uni the Unicorn remained pensive for a while, then slowly began moving westwards, into Europa. He had at last come to terms with a certain understanding of himself, and he had an old Owl to thank for this. Now maybe he could get along with his life without worrying too much about who he was, where he'd come from, and why he had been chosen to be Memory. At least for the moment….

Part 4

CHAPTER 21
Ecclesia

It was now over thirteen hundred years A.D., and the Unicorn saw Ecclesia in a sorry state indeed. Although it was an age of great piety, of pilgrimages to the holy places of Christianity, and of the construction of magnificent Cathedrals all over Europa, yet for over two hundred years corruption reigned in the place of charity and sound teaching. The selling of Dioceses, Parishes and entire monasteries and their benefits to the highest bidder continued at a furious pace, absenteeism among the Bishops was rampant, and many priests, Bishops – and even successors of the Fisherman – had forgotten their vows, above all that of chastity. There were cases of infant children of the Fishermen being appointed Cardinals or Bishops in their tender years. There were no Seminaries for the training of the clergy, and many were ordained with just the barest minimum of Christian teaching in their repertoire. Some had only a passing notion of the Bible.

Coupled to this treachery of the Child's teaching, Islam was also making swift inroads into Christianity. Several countries more were overcome by force, and in the Mediterranean Turkish pirates made life hard for sea-going Christian merchantmen. This led to alliances and leagues being formed among the emerging nations of Europa, and Ecclesia herself got into the act. With the help of the Italian Princes, her forces fought a decisive victorious battle at sea off the Italian coast of Lepanto (a) against the ships of the Muslim Turks. After this there was a slowing down of Islamic expansion into Europa, and it appeared to Uni that this would be an end of the direct attacks of Islam against Christianity. He was wrong, as later history showed…...

Great Saints came to the fore in those dark days – the Unicorn heard people speaking of a certain little Poor Man at Assisi in Italy (b), and of the founder of an Order of wandering Preachers (c), whose efforts to reconvert the south of France were bearing marvellous fruit, as well as of others who were pushing for reform in Ecclesia. But she was agonisingly slow to harness her spiritual forces, and the rot continued from the interior, while Islam continued to pile on the pressure masterfully from the outside. From being an Eastern religion to be merely tolerated, Islam had become known as the Enemy, as the main menace to Christianity. The answer to this had been the unleashing of the armies of the Crusades, which overall had been a failure (d).

81

The incident which had the most heart-rending effect upon Western Christianity, and upon the Unicorn, was the fall of Constantinople, the Eastern half of the former Roman Empire (e). The taking of the city by the Ottoman Turks was followed by the wholesale massacre for three days of thousands of Christians, whose throats were cut as they prayed fervently in their immense Cathedral, Saint Sophia. More than fifty thousand Greek Christians of both sexes and of all ages were sold into slavery, and Saint Sophia was later converted onto a mosque.

This disaster was only compensated in part when, at the very end of the 15th century, Muslim domination of the Spanish Peninsula ended (f), and their peoples retreated into north and western Africa. But five years before this a Portuguese navigator had already rounded its southern tip (g).

In the same year of the liberation of Spain from Islam a certain hired navigator (h) reached the Western Hemisphere in three little ships (i), and the race was on to acquire as much territory as possible. The kingdoms of Portugal and Spain risked coming into conflict because of territorial claims, and this was only avoided be the intervention of the Fisherman at the time, whose personal life was itself far less than a model of sanctity (j). He divided the globe into zones of influence between them.

But the continuing clamours for reform against abuses in Ecclesia fell on deaf ears, and soon a German monk (k) protested by mailing his "95 Theses" to the Bishop of the diocese where he served. He was soon followed by several others of different tendencies (l), and the Protestant Reformation was thus set in motion.

Events followed swiftly, and soon this movement spread throughout Europa. But it became increasingly clear to Uni that these "Reformers" wanted not merely to correct abuses in the Ecclesia-Mother, but above all to start new and local ones, which in fact is what happened. In Germany the movement became national (m), and so did it also in Switzerland and neighbouring States (n).

It took Ecclesia a long time to get moving, but eventually after nine years of preparation, amid formidable harassment by opponents of reform against the Fisherman of the moment at Roma, a Council was summoned at last in Italy (o). This met in several cities over this period, and lasted for eighteen years, but the real Reform of Ecclesia had finally begun. With all the movement of clergy around Europe, the Unicorn could not but be aware of the importance of these meetings.

Simony, nepotism, concubinage by the clergy, lack of discipline in convents and monasteries, the absenteeism of Bishops from their Dioceses, and accumulation of the same by Prelates, were all blocked and legislated for in a new Code of Canon Law, and directions for the setting up of Seminaries for the correct formation of priests were issued.

In her efforts to reform, Ecclesia was helped by the newly-founded Society of Jesus (p), which worked hard to put into concrete form the Council's decrees, and by the Order of Preachers and the followers of Francis of Assisi. One of the most eminent of the time was an Italian Jesuit (q), founder of Seminaries and promoter of diocesan missionaries.

Not content with merely winning back the errant Christian countries, these Orders went all out in a new effort to evangelise the pagans, in the Far East (r), in the Americas (s), and in Europa itself.

But this was not to say that the countries-turned-Protestant looked upon these brave men with an indulgent eye. Many were martyred, suffering the most terrible deaths that the executioners could devise. And there were serious excesses also on the part of those Princes who had remained faithful to the cause of Ecclesia (t). But she had found her true role again, and continued to send out her missionaries, knowing fully well into what terrible dangers she was engaging them

At this time wars began between the Princes faithful to Ecclesia and those of the Reformation in various parts of Europa, and to the Unicorn it became clear that her unity had gone. Whereas four hundred years before a form of international identity had been lived among these peoples, where passports were not necessary, and where the intelligentsia, students, clerics, and merchants moved around freely from place to place, Europa had become a quite different world after the catastrophe of the Protestant Reformation.

Chapter 22
Squabbles

The first war lasted for thirty years (a), and Uni wondered what could be done for Europa to find her unity again. The Protestant Reformers could never have succeeded had not the self-seeking Princes supported them. But the damage had been done, and Europa had broken apart. *Would she ever find her way together again?* mused the Unicorn.... *Would she even want to?*

From the Russian interior also, the news was not good at all for the unity of Ecclesia. The continued schism between the successors of the Eastern Empire in Constantinople (b), and Ecclesia continued to rankle. The former were still angry and bitter at the massacres of fellow-Christians that the Crusaders had committed in Constantinople, much later to be called Istanbul by the Turkish Ottomans. The deep spiritual traditions of the East had gone north, first to Greece and then to Moscow, after the fall of the Second Roma, as Constantinople had considered herself to be.

Although many Christians continued to live among the Faithful of Allah in Istanbul as protected *"dhimmi"*, paying their *"jizya"* taxes to be allowed to practise their own Faith, many had in fact accepted Islam to avoid the heavy taxes and social ostracism. All these factors remained to embitter the followers of the Eastern Rite, and so they kept to their own ways, and remained separated from the main body of Ecclesia, thus keeping alive the excommunications that each had pronounced upon the other (c). Positions had in fact finally become hardened both by the high-handed attitude of Ecclesia at Roma, which had been slow to put charity and understanding to work, and by the intransigence of the Eastern Christians of Moscow.

So as to find out for himself the truth of these stories which he'd heard of, the Unicorn found his way to Greece and then to Russia, both firm bastions of Eastern spirituality, and marvelled at the peace that seemed to reign there. He was impressed by the processions, the sacred Rites, the love for the Resurrected Child. These people seemed to take their Faith and vows seriously, nothing seemed to be like the squabbling and infighting which he had observed in Europa.

But he also saw that these States protected the Easterners exactly as Constantine had done to the young Ecclesia in the fourth century A.D. They had a major say in the internal affairs of their religion, appointing Bishops favourable to its policies, manipulating its decisions to its own ends. To Uni the Easterners seemed like the proverbial bird in the gilded cage, while Ecclesia in Roma was independent of Princes and governments, at least in principle. She had fought hard for this independence, even at the cost of alienating her own supporters.

So, he took the road back to Europa, happy to have experienced another form of Christianity. But what would the Child have made of such divisions? he thought. His message of mutual love and pardon seemed to have been lost…

In the meantime, Islam was again proclaiming its belligerence. Just over a century after its defeat in the sea battle against the Christian navy, its forces again attacked the West, almost taking Vienna, but were stopped at the very gates of the city by the Christian army of Poland (d), and then run out of Hungary. Coming after the golden age of Islamic culture (e), the Unicorn saw these events as signs of a definite decline in Islamic importance in world affairs.

Remembering that most of the present countries under Muslim rule were once Christian, which had been conquered and their peoples more or less forcibly converted, Uni came to the conclusion that "Allah, the Clement, the Merciful, the Compassionate", possessed these attributes only insofar as relating to the people of the Koran. He saw Muslims as being absolutely convinced of the superiority of their religion in relation to that of other peoples. They would not tolerate co-existence with those of other Faiths, unless they were in the minority. If in the majority, there would always be subtle pressure on the others to convert, using the *"jizya"* tax system, the denial of influence in public affairs, the obligatory conversion of wives upon marriage, and Islamic education for their children. Conversion to other Faiths was forbidden by Islam as treason, punishable by exclusion from the Community of Believers, boycottage of businesses, exile, even death. And the few Muslims who converted to Christianity were forcibly divorced from their wives, thereby losing also their children.

The Unicorn saw Islam as a perfectly iron-clad system, believing sincerely in itself and denigrating all others as second-class believers, or even considered as idolaters. All was in their Holy Koran, dictated by Allah Himself, and transmitted to His faithful Prophet, *"Peace be upon him!"*. *"Mekhtub!"*, *"It is written"*, the Believers would say, and sincerely believe it. All world history, past present and future, was there in the Holy Koran for him who has eyes to see and ears to hear. No criticism of their Book was ever to be permitted. Religious freedom was alien to its ethos.

And yet, mused the Unicorn, Islam is a small part, yet an important part, of history. The world changes, people change, history moves on. The irrevocability of the written word may yet prove to be a serious drawback. His thoughts were to prove prophetic……

On her side, Ecclesia also had her bouts of intolerance and self-righteousness, as did the Protestant Kingdoms which had thought to do away with the authority of the Fisherman and many of the Articles of Faith of Ecclesia. At times their seemingly irreconcilable positions burgeoned into conflict; bloody engagements ensued with each side eliminating their adversaries by war, public executions of varying degrees of barbarism, or even by State-inspired massacres (f). In these engagements both sides sinned gravely, thought the Unicorn, for not having tempered whatever righteousness of opinion they had with the precept of Christian charity, as taught by the Child. An attempt to adjust to the reality of having both followers of Ecclesia and Protestants in the same kingdom was carried out in France, but was abandoned less than a hundred years later, causing untold damage to national identity and inter-confessional tolerance, among other things (g).

The problem of maintaining national identity was everywhere in those days when Europa was in full disarray, each nation trying to find itself after the break-up of Christian unity. Uni saw this as being most evident in Spain. Having liberated herself from Islam after nearly eight centuries of Muslim rule (h), she now faced the problem of preserving her newly-found national unity and internal peace, in great danger of being compromised by the presence of Protestant groups on her territory, with all the proselytism that that involved.

The Iberian monarchs turned for help to the Office for the Discovery of Heresy, put in motion by Ecclesia after the great reforming Council (i), even though it had existed long before (j). This Office became a Ministry on Spain, and heretics were ruthlessly hunted out, had to recant or suffer exile. Some were executed publicly, and Protestant worship was forbidden. While this had the effect of protecting the Spanish State and Ecclesia, yet Uni saw her as being manipulated by the State for purely political ends. Unfortunately, her role in pursuing national necessity would in future years be levelled against Ecclesia as intolerance by her adversaries.

Yet once again, Uni had to admit, while keeping an open mind, that the actions of the Reformers, and even of Ecclesia, often did not seem to be based on charity nor unity, but rather on their opposites. He had once seen an *auto-da-fé* in Spain, when thousands of books, pamphlets and other Protestant literature were publicly burnt, to be soon followed by their promulgators. It had not been a pretty sight, and the smell of burning flesh would forever remain with him. And yet, given the brutality of the age and the bitterness over lost unity, could there have been other adequate means of avoiding teaching which would threaten State cohesion and social order?

Though he had never visited the island of Britain, yet occasional contact with mounts brought to the continent by their owners informed him that Protestantism, born during the recovery of the ancient cultures of Greece and Roma, had been solidly implanted in that island, the King having forced the Parliament to recognize him as Supreme Head of the State, and even of Ecclesia there (k). She was thus outlawed, and in the ensuing persecution many native Bishops and Religious Superiors, monks and clergy were exiled, or decapitated. The great monasteries were suppressed, the monks dispersed, their properties sold off for a song to the suddenly ennobled wealthy. The King had need of money for his wars, and the lead from the monastery roofs for his cannon-balls…The Lord Chancellor of the Kingdom paid with his life for his temerity in criticizing the monarch (l), as well as some of the leading Bishops. *"Cherchez la femme!"* thought Uni, with his mind on the six wives of the King, cause of all his troubles (m), as the Monarch himself is supposed to have admitted.

Subsequent Kings and Queens of Britain either sought to reinstall Ecclesia or to outlaw her (n), but the latter prevailed, and the followers of the Old Faith became a heavily-taxed, a socially- discriminated-against people, a persecuted people, as in the first centuries under the Roman Emperors….a sorry repetition of history…(o).

The Unicorn could only look on and wonder how all this would end. But of one thing he was sure – Europa would never be the same again.

CHAPTER 23

Century of Light.

With the arrival of Protestantism came also the time known as the Enlightenment, urged on enormously by the use of the printing-press. A practical way of using movable type had seen the day in Germany (a), and the Bible became the first book to be printed. Suddenly there arose tremendous interest in the world of the ancients. Uni saw the statues of ancient Roma and Greece being unearthed and repaired; the monuments cleaned of the accumulated crass of centuries. Works of the Greek and Roman philosophers, playwrights, poets, were all brought to light again and studied by enthusiastic thinkers in Europa. Ancient works were reprinted, distributed, commented upon in all the important Universities, and little by little this new interest filtered down to the general public who looked, some to Ecclesia, some to their Protestant mentors, for guidance. These were heady times, and Uni could feel the tension as new methods of understanding the world emerged from Man's curiosity.

The experimental sciences also had a new beginning. The early theory that the Earth was the centre of the universe was challenged by a Polish scientist and cleric (b), and this was further corroborated by the observations of the Italian inventor of the telescope, Galileo (c).

Uni wondered what Ecclesia had to say about all these new developments. Would she accept them, or reject them? After all, she had been the guardian of learning for so long, and these new ways would no doubt be seen as a direct challenge to her authority.

At first Ecclesia looked askance at these new ways of considering the universe, and then unfortunately condemned them instead of taking the time to see their value. She took a wrong turn again, basing herself on the literal interpretation of her Bible that the Earth is the centre of the universe, that Joshua himself had arrested the Sun's movement (d).

Galileo was arrested for his theories and unfortunately defended himself by also quoting the Bible, which was the same as questioning the authority of Ecclesia, one of the main precepts of the Protestant Reformation. He was suspected of heresy, in an Italy whose rulers wanted nothing to do with Protestants in their country, and was eventually kept under house arrest for some years. He was later released after his work and theories had been examined and found free of error.

But the damage had been done, and Uni saw Ecclesia branded as anti-intellectual by the Protestants of the Enlightenment. The presumed row between Science and Faith had started on a false footing, and would last for centuries (e).

Ecclesia also looked with a wary eye at the new thinking, and saw in it the very solid germs of agnosticism and atheism. To her the Enlightenment was a largely pagan movement, abnormally liberal, disdaining authority, and obsessed with the ancient pagan philosophers Aristotle, Democritus, Socrates, Plato, and their like, while ignoring the Christianisation of thought through the centuries based upon those very philosophies by Ecclesia herself (f). She saw herself as the guardian of truth for those in her charge, and therefore entitled to defend her position in no uncertain terms.

Another Italian (g) though a faithful follower of Ecclesia, had suggested that "A Prince, in order to preserve unity in his kingdom, could justifiably put aside the principle that *the end does not justify the means*". To her way of thinking, this, if put into practice, would justify the political powers supporting the Protestant Reformation, and this only served to put Ecclesia's back up against the wall.

Yet there were also Christian humanists, as they came to be called, and the most famous of them all (h) broke with the greatest of the Reformers (i) once he had realised that the renewal would not be within the ancient Ecclesia, but a naked bid to create a totally new one. To the Unicorn this was a sign that the wish to retain some semblance of unity in Europa had not entirely died.

CHAPTER 24
For Better or Worse.

Starting from this Century of Light, dramatic events came to shake Western society. Colonisation and settlement of the Americas had seriously begun, with its attendant evils of African slavery, the genocide of the copper-men of the North American plains, and the destruction of the native empires of Central and South America (a).

From the information he was able to glean around the sea-ports and big cities of Europa, the Unicorn came to estimate that over thirty millions of African men, women and children had been dragged from their continent and sold into slavery in the Americas, both North and South. The trade was being run industrially by the usual Islamic States, and by at least eight Christian countries whose Faith, whether of Ecclesia or Protestant, failed before the lure of fabulous earnings through black labour. The sad part was that many had been sold into slavery by their own unscrupulous leaders....

For great fortunes were generated both in the Americas and in Europa through slavery, and several of the greatest cities owed their rapid growth and wealth to this infamous commerce. Sadly, Ecclesia lost control once again, and though great Saints and an occasional Bishop protested or helped the slaves in their great distress, yet Ecclesia could not enforce its official pronouncements.

It was from the schismatic groups of Protestant Christians that the first real consciousness of the evils of slavery took hold. Once liberal thinkers had become convinced of the innate inhumanity of slavery, Christian values of charity towards others prompted certain wealthy British (b) to influence Parliament, and in time slavery in British territories was outlawed (c), after pressure groups had been formed. The anti-slavery movement took root elsewhere, and other countries followed suit. Soon the trade *officially* was over, having flourished for four hundred years, the cause of untold suffering. But it would continue for awhile still, in the largest Christian country of all (d), and in many Islamic States it continued with no hindrance whatsoever......

Once the authority of Ecclesia had been challenged and rejected, most of the States of Europa went their own political ways, building up their own armies and waging wars unchecked. The moral high ground imposed by Ecclesia in the past had been lost.

The Thirty Years War (e) had proved this point, to the great dismay of Ecclesia, but events became more serious among the Protestant nations themselves, starting with the revolt of Britain's American colonies (f). This was partly based on French philosophy (g), partly on their not being represented in the British Parliament, although being heavily taxed on imports from Britain. This Revolution was encouraged by France, wishing to even the score with her old enemy for past humiliations and losses in war (h). The Unicorn saw the French troops leave for the American colonies, learned of the ending of British rule there, saw the ships return to France, heard in the bars the tales of battles won, of the British being chased from American soil. *Vive l'Amérique! Vive la France!*, as the matelots clinked their mugs of beer and swigged their wine under a cloud of smoke.....

In France itself this had been preceded by a return of absolute authority, in the person of the Sun King (i), and Uni followed with amazement the accomplishments of this man, including the endless series of wars which marked his reign. Versailles with its Hall of Mirrors and its immense park with wild deer roaming freely was just one of his wonders, and Ecclesia prospered under him. Perhaps too much – for the poor became poorer, and deep resentment bubbled beneath the surface. His long reign had exhausted the country, and two generations later came to the surface, with disastrous results.

The flame of revolution which had begun in the British colonies of America spread to France (j), egged on this time by the British – "perfidious Albion" for later generations of Frenchmen. Dame Guillotine regularly rose and fell in the subsequent upheaval, and every fall meant a head lopped off. King and Queen (k), nobles, bourgeois, priests, religious men and women, "enemies" of the Revolution, and eventually the leaders themselves (l), all bowed down at least once before this terrible Lady, never to rise again. Nor did the "Ancien Regime". For better or worse, people had changed.

In the ensuing confusion a certain tubby little Corporal from Corsica (m) took charge, raised armies to stabilise the country, and proceeded to conquer most of Europa, parts of the Middle East and Egypt. He crowned himself Emperor in Paris, undertook the conquest of Russia, was defeated by that country's best ally – Lord Winter, and had to retreat ingloriously across the icy wastes.

He then lost to the British and their allies in Europa, surrendered and was exiled (n), escaped, raised another huge army, lost again to the British and Prussians (o), and finally died in exile in his own little mid-ocean island-Kingdom (p).

France had invited the world to its Revolution party, but it had gone sour on her, and to the Unicorn it seemed that the country was worse off afterwards, than before all those sad events.

In the meadows of Europa where he found life easier than in the bustling cities, the Unicorn often retired to think again of all these tremendous changes taking place there. It was clear to him that the old Europa and its internal unity had gone, that it was now more a question of alliances and economic interests among individual nations that dominated the scene, not obedience to any higher authority in view of the common good. Moral leadership indeed continued to come from Ecclesia, but she was obeyed only in the countries where she still had influence.

The various breakaway Protestant groups had further sub-divided into several smaller entities, none of which presumed to assert itself as a criterion for the rest. Some of these latter were in fact persecuted by the older established ones, and Uni saw one particular group (q) flee to North America, so as to be able to worship as they wished.

In the various newly-formed nations of Europa the thirst for domination by the strongest succeeded to the moral restraints formerly imposed by the Ecclesia of the Child of Bethlehem, and governments rose and fell as alliances were made and broken, as national interests ebbed and flowed.

In Britain, Royalty had been ousted (r), the country had then first become a Republic (s), then was reinstalled as a Kingdom (t), and eventually settled into being a constitutional monarchy.

The Revolution in France had definitely finished off the monarchy there, apart from two brief attempts at Restoration (u), and slowly a certain democratic process "of the people, by the people, for the people" began to emerge (v), and the concept of a Republic slowly took form.

Other countries followed their various political choices, but it became clear to Uni that a free-for-all where morality in politics took a poor second place seemed to be now the norm.

In the meantime, the little island-Kingdom of Britain was fast becoming the most far-flung Empire the world had ever known, and in the ports of Europa the Unicorn learned that in fact the countries eventually controlled by this Empire had completely encircled the globe. It stretched from Africa to the Middle East, to India, to Australia, New Zealand and the South Seas, to certain Central American countries, to the islands of the Antilles, then across the Ocean and so back to Britain. It was said that "the sun never set on it….". But then again Uni had not visited all the lands of which he was now becoming aware…

All this of course did not go down too well with the other countries of Europa, and especially so with France, her arch-enemy of old. Economic competitiveness set in, with sniping and underhand dealings coming from both sides. Other countries were content to sit back and let the giants battle it out. Ecclesia had more or less closed in upon herself, licking the wounds of the Reformation and putting into effect the far-reaching decisions of her own Reform as decided by the great Council.

In all this turmoil, the Unicorn decided not to return to the Far East, to India, China and Japan. Europa was the place where things were happening, while from the snippets of information he gleaned here and there he learned that the Eastern half of the world had remained almost just as he had left it so long ago, locked up in its polytheism and navel-gazing. But he decided to go southwards to what the people of Europa were calling the "Dark Continent". To Africa. He had been there many centuries before, and remembered clearly the kingdoms of the Pyramid-Builders, as well as the regions to the west of these. *"Had there been changes?",* he wondered.

CHAPTER 25
Africa

Swimming the thin neck of water from Gibraltar to the African mainland was simple, and Uni wandered for many weeks along the northern coast, taking in the sights and experiences as in the past. He learned from the beautiful horses in their corrals that no followers of the Child now lived there, all had been wiped out by the Warriors of Allah. Of churches in ruin there were plenty, many had been converted into Islamic prayer-houses, others destroyed. The very monotony of these countries depress-ed the Unicorn, and so he took to the caravan trails across the desert, to see what lay to the south.

In a mud city called Timbuktu he visited the enormous fortress-like mosque, saw the crowds at prayer, heard the muezzin calling the faithful at early dawn, watched the children in their *madrasas* (a) chanting out the lessons of the Koran in Arabic, the verses scribbled on their writing-boards. He marvelled at such organization and close-knit unity, a far cry from the rivalries and turmoil of Europa.

And he saw the same phenomenon at another mud-city called Djenné, another at Mopti, and heard of others farther to the south and to the east and west. The Muslim world had indeed been solidly planted in these West-African countries, he concluded.

But apart from these efforts to teach the Word of Allah to the already converted, and a subtle pressure on the black populations to convert, Uni saw no progress at all. The peoples of the *bilâd as-sûdân* (b) continued making their sacrifices to their fetishes in their sacred groves, and were continually raided by the Muslim traders in search of slaves. No civil schools had been set up, hospitals and medical care were unknown, sickness and death were rife, widespread ignorance and superstition reigned. Of social services, government, administration, organization, visions of the present with planning for the future, there were none.

This situation seemed to have existed for many centuries, the Unicorn concluded. Even though Islamic influence could have had a salutary effect on the black African populations, yet absolutely nothing had been done to promote progress and new thought. In fact, the great social changes, the development of culture and the emer-gence of new philosophies in the countries of Europa to the north – which had in fact been given an important impetus by enlightened Muslim philosophers (c) – had gone completely unperceived by these black populations to the south of the Great Desert, impeded as they had been for long centuries by the all-pervading Islamic presence. Time had literally stood still in this part of the world.

It was about this time that the countries of Europa began to seriously interest themselves in Africa. They had become rich due to the slave trade in former centuries, but now that that source of income had dried up due to an increased understanding of human rights, they busied themselves with consolidating their gains and developing their sciences, literature, general culture and knowledge. Great wars had been fought on their soil, great inventions had increased their mobility and possibilities, but the continent to the south remained largely, still, the «Dark Continent».

And so, they began sending out their explorers to the south to investigate this continent and its possibilities (d). The British, French, Italians and Germans financed expeditions to sound out the interior and its peoples. The Unicorn came across these little caravans from time to time, some with Arabic speakers so as to allay Islamic suspicions, others well protected by armed soldiers and with a hundred or more porters. They were all white folk, but he preferred to thought-speak with the animals of the caravans, avoiding contacts with the porters, whose superstitious nature could have given him away. But the pack animals knew nothing or very little about where the white folk had come from, where they going, or what they were looking for. They were mere pack animals, trained to obey....

It was far to the East of the vast continent that Uni came upon a gaunt white man in a small tent, writing on a little folding table late at night. An oil lamp shed a pale-yellow light upon his note-pad, and mosquito-netting kept the many bugs and beetles from entering his refuge. So, in the dusky night Uni touched his horn to a stone and stood beside the tent as he thought-spoke to the man.

Do not be afraid, white man, you cannot see me in the dark. May I speak with you, in your mind?

He saw the man give a slight start in wonder and surprise. The Unicorn continued.

Please be calm. I mean no harm, and you seem a man of courage. Would you tell me your name? Where are you from?

The man thought-spoke slowly in reply, unaccustomed to this form of communication. *I am David Livingstone, from Scotland (e). But who are you?*

* I am the One-Horn from the legends, but I am no legend. I am real, David, and I would like to know why you are here, and what you are doing*.

I was sent by the Church Missionary Society in England, to fight the Arab slave trade, and to bring the Good News of Jesus to the black folk here. I suppose you know about Jesus?

I am very old, David, and if he is the Child of Bethlehem, yes, I know him. I had been able to speak with him personally, many centuries ago. And I have followed the fortunes of his Ecclesia down through the ages, as best I could. Much of her history has been very sad, he added.

Yes, One-Horn, but maybe one day we will be one again, as my Church left Ecclesia three hundred years ago. She seemed to us to have forgotten Jesus…...

Could this not be that this was only apparent, a test from «He-Who-Is», and that things had been put right by the Great Council?

So you know of the Great Council too? Absolutely amazing! But yes, it could have been a test. But the Council came late, and now we are separated.…

How long do you expect to stay here, David?

I am a doctor and a missionary, One-Horn, and I see no need to return to my country as long as I can be useful here. Perhaps you don›t understand, but I love these people. They are basically very good, and are seeking the Truth which I hope to give them. So I suppose that I will remain here until I am recalled home, or until the Lord calls me.…

The Unicorn paused. He had no need to question the man any longer, so he spoke once more as he prepared to leave the missionary to his work.

I thank you for sharing with me your faith and hope, Doctor David Livingstone. I wish you well in your work, and now I will leave. May «He-Who-Is» accompany you.…

He cantered away slowly among the sleeping porters, while David Livingstone came outside and looked into the darkness. But the blue haze was invisible in the dark, and already a good way off. Livingstone shook his head in wonder, and re-entered his tent. He closed his note-book, and fell to his knees……

• • •

Basing itself on the reports of the many expeditions and explorers to the African continent, a Congress of some of the developed nations of Europa (f) was held in Germany almost at the end of the 19th century (g), and it was decided by these people that Africa should be colonised systematically, as up to then the countries of Europa had been entrenching themselves mainly along the coast, while the interior had been left largely untouched. It was to have served the continent, but basically it was also a means of balancing out any possible rivalries looming among the developing nations of the north.

The Islamic nations were not invited to this Congress, and so were surprised when news of this decision reached them. They realized that they would be in danger of being ousted from the continent where they had lived in immunity for so many centuries. They would lose all their benefits, especially their gains from sales in the slave trade, still rampant throughout the continent, if the nations of Europa began poking their noses into their affairs.

As could have been expected, Muslim hostility arose to these foreign incursions into territories hitherto considered Islamic strongholds, whether in East or West Africa, and when the northern nations began entering into and taking possession of the lands they had so gratuitously carved up for their own benefit, they met with stiff resistance for some time from local Islamic armies and guerrillas (h), as well as from the chiefs and kings of the countries taken over (i).

Observing these events, the Unicorn could not but help thinking that now the shoe was on the other foot. Islamic armies had done the same thing many centuries ago to the whole of North Africa, as well as to many countries in the Near and Middle East, during their conquest in the name of their new religion, Islam.

The majority of these same countries and their peoples had hitherto been faithful to Ecclesia, but had finally given in to pressure from their conquerors and converted to Islam, some through fear for their lives, some by the lure of economic gain, some by dislike of social ostracism or being considered "protected", and having to pay an humiliating tax for this privilege. Many had done so through pure ignorance of Islamic reality. There had been many who had died for their Faith, but not all had been called upon to take that road...

These pockets of resistance were eventually mastered, the leaders sent into exile, imprisoned, or killed in battle, and the colonisation of Africa began in earnest. The Unicorn saw the French, German, British and Portuguese arrive in droves to set up their businesses, government administration and services, as well as tax-collection structures. Schooling, health, social services, the Army, all were modelled on lines found workable in Europa. Ecclesia and the Protestant groups arrived in their turn, and set to work to teach the indigenous peoples the Good News and so bring them into the fold.

Uni saw the missionary efforts of these various followers of the Child of Bethlehem either eagerly accepted or haughtily rejected by different peoples. Both in the East and in the West, Mission schools and classes in religion were in general accepted by the simple black folk, who were encouraged to leave their wooden and stone fetishes behind and follow the liberating Child, the Messiah. When the parents discovered that the whites were not there to eat their children but to educate them, the rate of school-building could hardly keep pace with the increased demand for places. There was further excite-ment when it was realized that education would give the children and youth good jobs and responsible positions in the colonial administration, in the professions, and even posts in the Army...

But Islam sulked and kept its children away, fearing conversions to the Christian faith. When its leaders realized that their children were being left behind, they began coming out of their shells, and soon began sending their own children to these Mission schools. But they were ten or more years too late, and young Christians were soon taking over leading roles in civil society, more or less lording it over their Islamic neighbours.

Colonisation continued willy-nilly, and the Unicorn realised that the nations of Europa were not in Africa only for "the good of the Africans", but above all for their own. Whether British, French or whatever other Power was present, he saw agriculture, mining, lumbering and industry, and their modern methods, coming in and being applied. Would the Africans benefit from the materials found in their own countries, from the metals, woods, agricultural products? It was not to be....

Precious metals and stones, gold, diamonds, chrome, iron, were mined and shipped out to Europa. Valuable timber was felled and exported. Tea, coffee, cacao, rubber, and various oil-bearing nuts were harvested, exported, then re-imported into Africa. To the great enrichment of the colonial powers, of course, and to a lesser extent, that of the colonised. In all this race to get rich, injustices were sure to be caused, and Uni saw the virtual enslavement of the "liberated" Africans by various unscrupulous colonial masters, who mutilated or killed with impunity those whose production was not up to expectations (j).

The ago-old slavery as practised by Islam in Africa was brought more or less under control, due to the untiring efforts of the modern "prophets" of the anti-slave Movements (k), and in some countries even ended. But the present alternative of unchecked greed and rape of the lands belonging to people unable to defend themselves against modern weapons seemed to make a mockery of colonisation claiming to be "for the good of the African peoples".

Or so concluded the Unicorn.......

CHAPTER 26

Wars

Uni had seen much suffering and death in the wars of past centuries, but these had been mostly affairs involving infantry, horses being reserved for the noble elite who could afford to upkeep them.

With the invention and proper use of gunpowder, however, bows and arrows, lances and heavy body-armour, both for men and horses, had become practically useless against the muskets, arquebuses and cannon of the new armies equipped with them. Just before colonisation had been decided upon in Germany, there had been a war between France and the emerging warlike Prussian States of Germany, with disastrous results for the former (a). Resentment simmered in French breasts.

Just a few years after the turn of the new century, the newly-invented aeroplane (b) was improved upon, and was soon seen as an ideal instrument for waging war from the air itself.

Hurrying back to Europa at the news of the outbreak of hostilities again between France and Germany, the Unicorn saw with horror the carnage and loss of a whole generation of European youth, with the onset of the improved means of modern warfare (c). Aeroplanes, tanks, battleships, sub-marines, and an infinite array of cannon and guns turned human beings to mincemeat as the armies flowed back and forth throughout Europa. Many more countries, thirty-five in all, had joined the fray on both sides – Britain, Turkey, Russia, France, and Italy included, and finally even the fledgling United States, hitherto vowed to neutrality.

Africans too from the Colonies joined up, and were slaughtered along with the rest. Bullets and shells made no difference between a white man, a brown man, nor a black. Uni mused that a bullet was proof of democracy in action….one man one vote, one man one bullet….

The Head of Ecclesia in Roma had done all that was possible in his power to keep the nations of Europa away from conflict, but had died of a broken heart at the outbreak of hostilities (d). The four years of what came to be called the Great War saw the map of Europa re-drawn, with over eight million killed, countless wounded, and untold damage done to the self-esteem of the European mind.

It also was the end of an epoch, the end of the old established order. This order had in fact been slowly dying over the past three centuries through the rivalries between countries swearing allegiance to Ecclesia and those of the break-away Protestant groups. The War had in fact been, like most wars, a conflict of economies, international rivalries, and jealousies over colonies and property, and had brought into play the old demons of domination and nationalism which Ecclesia had been able to contain in past centuries through her moral authority.

And during the War itself, the Russian Revolution (e) had thrown out the ruling Czars for ever. Socialism was born, based on the economic theories of a German communist (f), and put into political practice by unscrupulous movers of men (g). Thus, a new pawn was thrown onto the international checkerboard, the results of which would severely try the efforts of the brave and the good to make sense of a world which seemed to have lost its very direction.

When the madness had ended and the Peace Treaty had been signed (h), the Unicorn had believed that real peace would give Europa a chance to rebuild once again. But in this he was wrong. An obscure Austrian Army corporal (i) who had seen service in the Great War put paid to that dream, and once again dragged Europa, and the whole world with her, into the greatest conflict imaginable, the Second World War, just twenty-one years later. It was to last for six years (j).

This man, a failed artist whose paranoia concerning Teutonic superiority was fed by the bitterness of German defeat in the Great War and his personal megalomania, played upon the national sentiment of humiliation and a desire for revenge, and when a severe economic crisis took hold in Germany in 1929 – Uni had long become accustomed to using modern dates – he took over supreme power there as Chancellor. He organised an even more modern army, re-armed secretly against the terms of the Peace Treaty of 1919, and invaded Poland under false pretences (k), having tricked Britain and the whole world into believing that war was not imminent.

For six long years the Unicorn saw death stalk the world, no country being spared the effects of the war. From Europa to the Americas, from Africa to Russia, to China, the Middle and Far East, China, India, Japan, the world went mad. Over fifty-two million people died, six million of whom were Children of Abraham in death-camps organized by the executioners of *Der Fuhrer*, and under his orders. Human decency became a thing of the past as each side tried to outdo the other in destroying towns and cities, firebombing defenceless civilians, stoking the fires of hate where there should have been compassion and humanity. There seemed to be no real difference between the war in the East and that in the West, according to reports. Mankind had indeed sunk to depths of generalised savagery undreamed of in past centuries.

In all this cataclysmic upheaval, the Unicorn saw that Ecclesia was suffering as much as the people among whom she was working. Her priests were put into forced-labour camps, many would end their days there. Her religious daughters were not spared either, many dying in camps or on forced marches across the mountains of the Eastern front in particular. Tales of their heroism came in little snippets of information, in particular when they were sacrificed along with the ill in their hospitals or in the schools they were running. Some died as martyrs of the Child, offering their lives in place of others picked to face the firing-squads or the starvation cells.

But in all this Ecclesia continued her work of charity, sheltering the homeless, distributing food, and hiding the persecuted in homes and churches as pursuants approached. The Fisherman at Roma had set up a network of escape lines for the Children of Abraham, and in the crypts of his very Basilica in Roma several hundred of them found temporary refuge before they could be spirited away. And when Roma itself was bombed, he was there in his white robe, consoling and encouraging the disheart-ened people of the City, giving hope and praying for the end of the war.

The western theatre of the war ended in 1944 when the Allied forces invaded Normandy and linked with their Russian allies in Berlin, Germany. But it continued for some months again in the Far East between Japan and the United States, finally ending only after two nuclear bombs – a totally new type of weapon – were dropped on two Japanese cities (1), atomising over one hundred and fifty thousand people immediately. Japan capitulated unconditionally. It was time to pick up the pieces.

Wandering through the ruined cities of Europa after the cannons had fallen silent, the Unicorn was at a loss to explain what had happened. Once again Germany had been defeated, had become two Germanies in fact, and his heart sank as he saw the suffering of the people in its aftermath. No food, no warmth in the cold of winter, no shelter except in the ruins of a vanished world.

For once again Europa had been shaken to its very foundations, and the values that had once held it together – its common Faith, the sense of a common destiny, even with all the infighting through the centuries, its administration and laws based on Greek thought and Roman organizational genius – all these seemed to have disappeared.

Even more than the wanton destruction of its past history, the damage to its inner soul and identity seemed even more permanent, and the Unicorn wondered what would happen next, now that an entire young generation had again been wiped out. Where would the necessary work force for reconstruction and normal running of so many countries come from? Now that women had taken over so many male jobs in the war effort, would they be willing to go back to being mere mothers in hearth and home? And where would husbands be found for re-population? What to do about the orphans and the innumerable refugees and other homeless, above all the Children of Abraham rescued from the concentration camps in Europa?

His brain staggered under the weight of these problems and more. Would Europa be able to reconstruct itself, and would its leaders be far-sighted enough to plan more solidly for the future? He was at a loss to imagine what the next move would be.... or should be....

As if the last war and its suffering had not been enough, the Cold War now began between the Russian Socialist bloc and their former allies. It was a time of unheard-of tension between the Communist Socialists, led by the Soviet Union, and the Democratic Capitalists, headed by the United States, Britain, and several countries of Europa. A policy of containment was decided upon by the Capitalist bloc, resulting in the formation of the North Atlantic Treaty Organization, in reply to the actions of the Socialists intent on spreading the Communist ideals of Marx and Lenin. They had taken advantage of the post-war confusion to grab territory here and there throughout Europa, and had cast its influence into far-off countries through their triple offers of development, aid and armaments. Needless to say, the Capitalist bloc replied in same, and so there started a world-wide race between both groups to extend their influence and secure a following sympathetic to their ideologies.

This was the cause of the Korean War (m), when North Korea tried with Soviet help to impose Socialism upon the South, supported by the United States, and which ended in a stalemate. But elsewhere, China took the Socialist road (n), as did the far-off Antillean island of Cuba. The President of this sugar-state (o) had then allowed the President of the Soviet Union (p) to install nuclear missiles on his island, just a stone's throw from the mainland United States. This occasioned a naval blocus of Cuba by the U.S. Navy, and the Unicorn saw the relief on the faces of the people in Europa when the danger of nuclear war was narrowly avoided by the Soviets being forced to remove its missiles (q).

And he shared their grief when the American President was assassinated just a year later (r).

Shortly afterwards Vietnam went completely Socialist also, and a war was fought to try to bring her back into line (s). But then first the French, then the American forces, had to retreat ignominiously from there, outwitted by the clever leadership of the bearded ascetic old man (t) leading the soldiers in sandals, notwithstanding the vaunted military superiority of the two defeated countries. It was America's first-ever defeat in war…

Almost the only bright spot that Uni observed during these sombre years was the meeting in Jerusalem of the two Christian leaders of both Ecclesia and Orthodoxy, in which the mutual excommunications pronounced against one another in the eleventh century were solemnly lifted (t).

Flash points continued igniting around the world at constant but irregular intervals, in South America, India, Pakistan, Tibet, several African countries, Ireland…. The list seemed endless, and the Unicorn found it was not even necessary to go to a distant place to get some idea about the situation there. He had gotten into the habit of spending hours at the store windows as a blue haze absorbing the news and views at open-air television, and he had his pick of information from the many radio programmes he heard. But the news about wars ending or just about to start never seemed to change…

As the years passed, the Unicorn realized that great inventions and adventures had changed men›s lives for ever. Certain diseases, once a direct ticket to the grave, were fought and conquered by the new drugs developed since the Second World War (u). The highest mountain in the world had been climbed for the first time (v), television and radio and clever household appliances were now commonplace, automobiles had caught the general publics fancy, aeroplane travel was not only for the wealthy. Man had now walked on the moon many times (w), had brought back rock specimens from that world captured so many eons ago. The Unicorn saw the satellites in the sky, the sending-off of probes to the planets, and now he was witnessing the great migrations of people from poor nations to wealthier ones, and the problems that this was causing. Indeed, he even came to admire the obstinacy of these migrants, many of them illegal, to try to secure a better life for themselves and their families.

So, he kept on observing and recording his impressions, keeping in his infallible memory all that his experience taught him, all the information which he seemed able to automatically register and classify. What was he going to do with it all? Would his life ever really make any sense?

Upon a sudden urge he decided to make another visit to the land of the Chosen People. He was untiring as ever as he skirted the villages of Rumania, Albania, Serbia, Montenegro, Greece, Turkey, Syria, Lebanon, and Palestine until he finally came once again to where he had spoken with the Child.

A huge Basilica had been built over the grotto of the Birth, the large entrance had been reduced to a narrow door to discourage mounted riders, so many invaders having entered there on horseback in past centuries. He seemed once again to see the Child holding out his little arms to him, thought-speaking to him, *Go in peace, One-Horn*. And he did.

In Jerusalem he found again the place where the Child-Man-Messiah had suffered and died on the Cross, entering the Basilica as a blue haze when few pilgrims were about. He stood again at the foot of the rocky outcrop of the Skull, at the top of which the Cross had been planted. He visited the tomb where his Body had been laid to rest, where he had returned to life, according to the Faith of Ecclesia, the only reason for her whole life and thought and teaching. For which so many had died…

And he saw the mutual suffering that the Chosen People and the Palestinians were inflicting on one another. Just three years after the Second World War the United Nations (x) had permitted the former to return to their ancestral land, but having done so they had found it occupied by Muslim Palestinians and a vigorous Christian Community.

They then proceeded to elbow themselves in by force, and from that year to the present, the Unicorn observed, there had been sporadic fighting and war ever since. The most recent desperate acts were the suicide bombers coming from the Palestinian people. Not having anything to lose, self-inflicted death seemed to them to be a small price to pay, as long as they took some others with them on their final, fatal journey. Young men and women, fathers of families…voting with their lives…

In the tremendous pressures put upon them by the squabbling factions, the people of the Christian Community seemed to have no other choice but to leave and install themselves in other countries. With sadness the Unicorn saw the half-empty churches, the fear of the unknown written across the faces of the few who remained, yet hopeful that one day real peace would come again to the Land of the Promise made to Abraham. Ecclesia was still present in the Land of the Child, but her force lay in love and peace, not in the fearful and terrible things that were being done in the name of God…or Allah…

The blue haze entered the Dome of the Rock, through its graceful arches under the very noses of the unsuspecting guards, and came to the Rock itself, situated directly under the cupola. This was the very place where the old man had so very nearly sacrificed his terrified son, so many centuries before.

This Rock had once been in the interior of the Temple of the Chosen People, mused the haze, as he regarded the large outcrop pockmarked by the picks and hammers of pilgrims and souvenir-hunters throughout the centuries. A sturdy surrounding iron grill now protected it against further vandalism, and at one end he could see steps leading down to the small prayer-room under the Rock itself. He understood the people to say that it was the very first mosque of Islam.

In the Dome itself the haze admired the delicacy of the inscriptions in Arabic and the beauty of the columns supporting the Dome and the whole structure. Some still bore crosses near the tops of the decorated cornices, having come from the Christian churches destroyed by Persian invaders (y). Their magnificent columns had been used again by the Christian Byzantine architects employed by the Caliph who had conquered Jerusalem (z). Then he looked up and saw masons chipping away at the crosses, obliterating them. There would soon be no proof of their Christian origins….

The whole building breathed an aura of peace and prayer, and the haze understood why Palestinian Muslims would go to any lengths not to lose this holy building to the modern State of Israel. *"Did not Abraham slay the sheep here, instead of his son? Was it not from here that the Prophet had made his mystical nocturnal journey to the throne of Allah, according to our Islamic tradition?"*

And, according to the Hebrews, *"Was it not in this very place that Abraham "our father" had nearly sacrificed his son Isaac? Was it not here that Solomon had built our First Temple, that Herod had renovated the Second, built after our return from exile in Babylon?"*

If both these claims were true, reasoned the Unicorn, then how could such opposing traditions ever be reconciled? Would they not, like the invincible force meeting the immovable object, mutually eliminate one another? He looked hard at the Rock.

This Rock, he saw clearly, was the ultimate cause of the great division between these two cousins in the faith. It has served to separate them in the past, could it not now serve to unite them? It embodied the Promise made to the Patriarch Abraham, and he saw that compromise would be the only way for the two enemy-cousins to co-exist. Even though the Chosen People were to take possession of the country as a whole, and of this Rock in particular, yet there never would be peace in this Land, were such a thing to happen. There would arise guerrilla fighters from all the Islamic countries, and the present uprising would be as child's play compared to what would eventually ensue.

No, reasoned the Unicorn, compromise in the sharing of the ownership of the Rock would seem to be the only solution, which would mean a certain form of internationalisation, a voluntary relinquishing of rights to property by both parties, and a shared maintenance of the Rock and its facilities.

In fact, the whole esplanade where the Dome of the Rock is situated could become a place of prayer for the three monotheistic religions, Islam, Judaism, and Christianity, he reasoned, *all in the name of the One God whom the three Faiths claimed to adore.*

But would the leaders of these Faiths ever come to an agreement for such a a revolutionary idea to see the light of day?

For the moment he considered that the time was not yet ripe for such developments, and he left the Dome of the Rock as he had come, unseen.

It was time for him to return to Roma.

CHAPTER 27
Reflexions

And so, the Unicorn made his way back to where Western civilization had found one of the roots of its greatness. To Roma, where Ecclesia lived on its tiny bit of independent territory, in the very heart of the ancient City (a). He saw the immense Basilica with its two curves of columns, like giant arms embracing the world, and remembered the furore that its building had caused over four centuries ago. The Protestant Reformation had started here, in Roma itself, and this great building had been one of its causes.

But Reformation seemed to have become deformation, taking into account all the terrible things that had happened due to the divisions in Ecclesia and among the people of Europa since those days when Luther had mailed his "95 Theses" to the Bishop…and the multitudinous churches and sects which had sprung from the original six Churches of the Reformation.

Had it all been worth it? he asked himself, and lingered near one of the columns as he saw a crowd of ragged gypsies and their children cross the square and enter the building. He saw them kneel and raise their arms in prayer, with their eyes closed.

And then he understood. It wasn't the overwhelming size nor the beauty of the Basilica that mattered. It was a house of prayer, a proof of the maternal care of Ecclesia for even the very poorest of her children, end even the poorest could find themselves at home in the arms of their Ecclesia-Mother. Even though she had committed grave errors in the past, and probably would in the future, yet he understood that Ecclesia had never lost sight that the Fisherman was there to "feed the lambs, take care of the sheep". She had remained true to the Child and his message across the centuries, even though some of her leaders had fallen short of the trust placed in them.

And he understood that she had not been built for time, but for eternity.

He was dismayed and disappointed at the way ordinary human society had behaved itself over the last century. Even though there had been magnificent inventions of every conceivable use, vast improvements in the sciences, medicine and political thought, yet the last hundred years had also been the most destructive in the history of mankind. Great men and women had lit up the darkness for a while, yet the forces of the night seemed to have entered the very heart of man.

The ordinary human values of understanding, patience, dialogue, compromise, give-and-take, compassion, had not yet been learnt. Mankind still seemed intent on proving that "might is right", and fraternity seemed to have taken a poor second place. The present violent events in the Middle East, the threat of nuclear proliferation, the crushing of the poorer nations and of the indigenous forest tribes by the more affluent, all these seemed to bear out the sombreness of his mood as he made his way into the open moonlit meadows on the outskirts of the sleeping city. He needed to think this out as he stood alone in the clearing, a pale white figure gleaming in the soft light of the shining disc above.

CHAPTER 28
Return

It was then that the intense blue light found him again. He looked up startled as it bathed him in its warm eerie glow, and he remembered its soothing caress upon his body so many centuries ago. It had the same effect on him now as it had in the past, and he stood still as his whole body became as intensely blue as the light itself. It had come back to find him, and he unconsciously realised that his time on Earth had come to an end. Perhaps now he would find out the reason for his very life.

Soon he felt his body changing, the flesh becoming crystalline of an intense blue, and starting with his horn, the Unicorn became a solid mass of highly interacting blue crystals. He was more aware then ever of what he was and where he was going, and looked forward with eagerness as the crystals in his body began to rise on the beam, joined one to another in an unending line of interlocking blue.

The beam was calling him back to his real home, to join the original wandering crystals of the ancient world. He knew at once that all the knowledge stored in his crystals would go to increase the tremendous store of interplanetary knowledge already stocked there.

So, this is why he'd lived so long, so this was the reason for his being – to become part of the Memory of the Universe.

The Unicorn surrendered to the call of the Moon-Crystals in the ecstatic knowledge that all this would some day, in some way as yet unknown to him, be used for the good of beings as yet unborn, that the good and the bad experiences of his existence would find sense on some future date, that his life would not have been a waste of time.

The crystals rose up and up on the blue beam, gaining speed as it intensified. Soon the whole crystalline body of the Unicorn had left the Earth, and would shortly join the Mother-Crystals in their hidden crater on Little World. Faster and faster sped the blue crystals as the Moon passed overhead, and when the last had left the Earth, the blue beam was cut off as suddenly as it had come down.

Uni had gone home; his job was over.

"Ooh, Jimmy, look at that!", exclaimed the girl as she sat in the shadows with her boy-friend. He glanced up, and they both stared in amazement as the blue beam seemed to come down from the moon, and then just as suddenly was cut off.

"What on earth could that have been?" asked the girl in alarm.

"Perhaps a new kind of laser. The army is always trying out new ones. I wouldn't worry over it if I were you", said the boy.

But then they both looked up and wondered. What in fact *had* they seen?

THE END

REFERENCE NOTES

N.B.: All dates are A.D. ("Anno Domini"), except when B.C. ("Before Christ") is indicated.
Biblical references are from the Bible of Jerusalem. Occasional references are taken from the Koran.

PART 1

Ch.1 **Before: Big World; Before: Little World.**
p.3 (a) Approx. 15 billion years ago.
p.5 (b) Approx. 4 billion years ago.

Ch.3 **After: The Stuff of Legend.**
p.11 (a) Eskimos.
(b) Small Arctic whale, the male having a horn over 2m long.

PART 2

Ch.4 **Start.**
p.16 (a) Eohippus.

Ch.5 **Meteor.**
p.17 (a) Gondwanaland.
(b) 65 million years ago, at Chicxulub, Yucatan, Mexico.
p.19 (c) Coelacanths, King Crabs, scorpions, cockroaches, certain frogs.

Ch.6 **Restart.**
p.21 (a) Moa, *Aepyornis Max.*
(b) Olduvaï, Tanzania.
p.23 (c) Tassili rock-paintings, Algerian Sahara.

Part 3

Ch:14   **Community.**
p.52   (a) 313, the Edict of Milan.
   (b) 324-330
p.53   (c) Mt.28: 18-20

Ch.15   **Nestor.**
p.54   (a) Arius, priest of Alexandria –256-336.
   (b) Councils of Nicaea (325) and of Constantinople (381)
   (c) Synod of Alexandria (430), and Council of Ephesus (431).

Ch.16   **Messenger.**
p.57-58   (a) Is.53.
   (b) Mecca.
p.59-61   (c) Medina.
   (d) 632, in Medina.
   (e) 638.
   (f) 642.
   (g) 652.
   (h) "jizya", taxed on the "protected" Christians("dhimmi")
   (i) Gibraltar.
   (j) 711.
   (k) 732 – led by Charles Martel.
   (l) 781 years (711 – 1492).
   (m) 1492.
   (n) Timbuktu and Djenné, in Mali, among other places.
   (o) Al-Azhar, Cairo, Egypt, since 973.
   (p) Koran.
   (q) Shari'a Law.
   (r) Koranic school.

Ch.17   **Travels To The Sun.**
p.63   (a) China, land of Kung fu Tsau(around 550-440 B.C.)
   (b) Buddhist monks.
   (c) Siddharta Gautama (560-480 B.C.)
p.64-65   (d) "wrap-around" loincloth.
   (e) Japan.

Ch.18   **West Goes East.**
p.66-67   (a) Aztecs, Tarascos, Toltecs, Maya, Otomi, etc.
   (b) Tonatiuh, Tlaloc, Huitzilopochtli, etc.
   (c) Maize.

(d) The Bering Strait.

(e) The Atlantic Ocean.

Ch.19   **East Goes West.**

p.70   (a) Two-humped camels.

(b) See Ch.13, *ante*.

(c) Attila the Hun- 452.

(d) Pope Leo the Great, 440-461.

p.72   (e) Mother of God.

(f) "Believer" in Arabic.

(g) 1096.

(h) 1099-1187, then 1229-1244.

(i) Under Salah-eh-Din(Saladin).

(j) Michael Cerularius, Patriarch of Constantinople, was excommunicated by the Papal Legate in 1054. He at once did the same. This consummated the Great Schism

(k) From 1204 – 1261

(l) The Orthodox Byzantine Rite.

(m) 1212.

p.73   (n) E.g. "Mary the New, the "Nea" Church, destroyed by Persian armies in 613.

Ch.20   **Memory.**

p.75   (a) See Ch.5, *ante*.

p.76   (b) Epigraph under all the Surates (Chapters) of the Koran, except for Ch.9.

PART 4

Ch.21   **Ecclesia.**

p.81-83   (a) 1571.

(b) Francis of Assisi (1182-1226).

(c) Dominic Guzman (1170-1221).

(d) See p.36, *ante*.

(e) 1453.

(f) 1492.

(g) Vasco da Gama, 1487.

(h) Christopher Columbus.

(i) Santa Maria, Niña, Pinta.

(j) Alexander Vl (1492-1503)

(k) Martin Luther (1517).

(l) Melanchthon, Zwingli, Calvin, Bucer, Knox, etc.

(m) Lutheranism, the Lutheran Church.

(n) Under Jean Calvin (1509-1564)

(o) Council of Trent (1545-1563).

(p) Founder: Ignatius of Loyola (1491-1556).

(q) Charles Borromeo (1538-1584).

(r) Matteo Ricci (1552-1610) in China.

(s) Junipero Serra (Franciscan); Eusebio Kino (Jesuit) etc.(18th c.)

(t) Mary Tudor ("Bloody Mary")(1553-58), Massacre of St Bartholomew(1572).

Ch.22   **Squabbles.**

p.84-87   (a) Thirty Years War (1618-1648).

(b) The "Orthodox".

(c) In 1054.

(d) 1683, led by the Polish King, Jan Sobieski.

(e) Under Soliman 1er the Magnificent (1494-1566).

(f) Massacres at Wassy (1562), and of St Bartholomew (1572), both in France.

(g) Edict of Nantes (1598), revoked in 1685.

(h) 781 years, from 711-1492.

(i) See Ch.21, note(o), *ante*.

(j) The Inquisition, in 1199, against the Cathar heresy in southern France.

(k) Henry Vlll (reign 1509-'47), by the Act of Supremacy (1535).

(l) Thomas More (+1535).

(m) Catherine of Aragon, Anne Boleyn, Jane Seymour, Anne of Cleves, Catherine   Howard, Catherine Parr.

(n) Edward Vl, Mary Tudor, Elizabeth 1st, James 1st.

(o) Mt.10:17 – 22.

Ch.23   **Century of Light.**

p.88   (a) Gutenberg, in 1455.

(b) Copernicus, 1473 – 1543.

(c) Galileo 1564 – 1642.

(d) Jos.10: 12-14.

(e) An examination of the Galileo case is still going on, by demand of John-Paul ll in 1979.

p.89   (f) E.g. Thomas Aquinas (1255 – 1274).

(g) Machiavelli,(1469 – 1527).

(h) Erasmus of Holland,(1469 – 1536), a cleric who scarcely exercised his ministry.

(i) Jean Calvin,(1509 – 1564).

Ch.24   **For Better or Worse.**

p.90   (a) The Aztec, Mayan, and Incan Empires.

(b) Wilberforce, Buxton, *inter alia*....

(c) Canada (1803), England (1807).

(d) Brazil, until 1888.

(e) See Ch.22, note(a), *ante*.

(f) The American Revolution (1776).

(g) E.g.: Jean-Jacques Rousseau (1712 – 1778).

(h) Seven Years War(1756 – 1763).

p.91-92   (i) Louis XlV(1638 – 1715) – "I am the State".

(j) 1792.

(k) Louis XVl, Marie Antoinette.

(l) Danton, Robespierre, Desmoulins…

(m) Napoléon Bonaparte (1769 – 1821)

(n) Island of Elba (1814 – 1815).

(o) Waterloo (1815).

(p) St Helena, in mid-Atlantic.

(q) Puritans in New England (1620, "Pilgrim Fathers).

(r) Execution of Charles l(1649).

(s) 1649, under Oliver Cromwell (dictator, 1645 – 1658).

(t) Charles ll (1660).

(u) 1814 – 1815; 1830 – 1848).

(v) Montesquieu (1689 – 1755).

Ch.25   **Africa.**

p.94   (a) Koranic schools.

(b) "the country of the blacks".

(c) Avicenna (980 – 1037); Averroes (1126 – 1198).

p.95   (d) Burton, Caillié, Nachtigal, Brazza, and many others.

(e) David Livingstone (1813 – 1873), doctor, missionary, explorer.

p.97   (f) Britain, France, Portugal, Germany, Belgium.

(g) Congress of Berlin (1884 – 1885).

(h) **Samory Touré** (1837-1900), from Northern Guinea, defeated in 1898 after resistance around the *Niger River and the Ivory Coast*. Deported and died in Gabon.

(*In Senegal*):**Al Hadj Omar**(1870), **Lat-Dior Diop**(1882-1884), **Alboury Ndiaye**, **Mamadou Lamine Dramé**, **Amadou Bamba**(founder of the Islamic sect, the "Mouridiste"), **El Hadj Malick Sy** (of the Tidjane Brotherhood).

(*In Somalia*): Against the English (1839) – by **Sayyid Mohammed** ("the crazy Mullah").

(*In the Sudan*): Against the English (1882-1898) by **Mohammed-el-Mahdi** (the "Mahdi").

(i) (*In Angola*, at that time part of the Congo): by **A-Nzinga**(warrior-Queen, defeated in 1648, **Mani Kongo Garcia ll** (17° s), **Kimpa Vita**(+1706).

Strong resistance in the *Congo(Brazza)*, *Ghana*(**Prempeh, Ashanti**), *South Africa*(**Xhosa**, **Ndebelé**, **Zulus**(**Chaka**, then **Dingaan**) against the Boers; **Cetewayo**(against the English).

(*In Benin*): **Béhanzin** (King of Abomey, 1844-1906). Exiled in Martinique, then Algeria).

(*In Namibia*): Strong resistance by the **Herreros** against the Germans.

(*In Ethiopia*): **Menelik ll**, victorious resistance against Italians, 1896.

(*In Nigeria*): Strong resistance against the English by the **Nupe** and **Igbo**.

Resistance in *Guinea-Bissau, Kenya, Madagascar, Haute-Volta* (Dedougou, 1915).

p.98   (j) The Belgian Congo in particular, now the Democratic Republic of Congo.

(k) Card. Charles Lavigerie (1825-1892), Arbp St.Daniel Comboni (1831-1881).

Ch.26   Wars

p.99   (a) Franco-Prussian War, 1870.

(b) By the Wright brothers, at Kitty Hawk, 1903.

(c) World War l (1914 – 1918).

(d) St. Pius X, 1914.

p.100   (e) October, 1917.

(f) Karl Marx (1813 – 1883)

(g) Lenin (1870 – 1924), Trotsky(1879 – 1940).

(h) Treaty of Versailles, 1919.

(i) Adolf Schikelgrüber (Hitler,1889 – 1945)

(j) 1939 – 1945.

(k) 1st September, 1939.

(l) Hiroshima, Nagasaki.

p.101   (m) The Korean War (1950 – 1953)

(n) Under Mao Tsé Tung (1893 – 1976) on the 1st October, 1949.

(o) Fidel Castro (1927-2016)

(p) Nikita Krutschev (1884 – 1971)

(q) 1962.

(r) J.F. Kennedy (1917 – 1963)

(s) The Vietnam War (1964 – 1973).

(t) Ho Chi Minh (1890 – 1969).

(t) Paul Vl and Patriarch Athenagoras in Jerusalem, 1965 (Schism of 1054).

p.103   (u) Antibiotics in particular.

(v) Mount Everest in the Nepalese Himalayas (1953)

(w) Starting with Neil Armstrong (21-7-1969)

(x) International body founded in 1946, replacing the League of Nations, 1919.

p.104   (y) In 613, by Chroesus ll of Iran (591-628).

(z) In 638, by the Calif Omar.

Ch.: 27   **Reflexions**

p.106   (a) Due to the Lateran Accords between Pius lX and Mussolini in 1929.